EROTIC VICTORIAN
FAIRY TALES

Other books by Paul Tabori

Sneeze on a Monday
The Ragged Guard
Japanese Jeopardy
The Leaf of a Lime Tree
They Came to London
Bricks Upon Dust
Solo
The Frontier
Spider and Moonlight: *A Trilogy*
Two Forests
Uneasy Giant
Heritage of Mercy
The Talking Tree
Another David
Salvatore
Perdita's End
Lighter Than Vanity
Sun of My Night
Appointment in Andrait
Private Gallery
The Survivors
The Big Appetite
The Green Rain
The Cleft
The Doomsday Brain
The Invisible Eye
The Devil at Angel Falls
The Plague of Sanity
The First Time (NEL)
Social History of Rape (NEL)
Song of the Scorpions (NEL)
Erotic Edwardian Fairy Tales (NEL)

Erotic Victorian Fairy Tales

Paul Tabori

NEW ENGLISH LIBRARY
TIMES MIRROR

Several of these stories have appeared in *Playboy* and acknowledg-
ment is made to that magazine, with thanks.

P. T.

An NEL Original
© 1971 by Paul Tabori

*

FIRST NEL EDITION NOVEMBER 1971

*

NEL Books are published by
New English Library Limited from Barnard's Inn, Holborn, London E.C.1.
Made and printed in Great Britain by Hunt Barnard Printing Ltd., Aylesbury, Bucks.

45000930 0

Introduction

It was G. K. Chesterton who pointed out that, apart from the industrial revolution, the most important happening in nineteenth century England was a non-event. There was no equivalent of the French Revolution in Britain; instead a peaceful levelling took place, the great Victorian compromise. The aristocracy and the upper middle class reached a silent pact to rule and guide the country.

One of the decisively important consequences of this compromise was the adoption, both by the aristocracy and the court, of the customs, habits and forms of the middle class – almost as soon as Victoria succeeded to the throne in 1837. Her long reign, spanning more than six decades, was accounted the most moral and most 'modest' period of humanity. The Queen and Albert, the Prince Consort, lived a model conjugal life surrounded by a host of children, and in the shadow of their throne the seriousness, the religious intensity and the purity of the old bourgeois morality became mandatory. The licentiousness of the eighteenth century was banished completely. England, the paradise of drunkards, became a tea-drinking country.

This, of course, is only part of the picture – one side of the total image. Victoria's reign was the age of Dr Bowdler and all the little bowdlerisers; of the sheeted piano-legs and the absolute prohibition of any book, painting, play or public exhibition that could bring the slightest blush to a maiden's cheeks. The wages of sin were social ostracism; Christian charity did not extend to sexual offences. Unmarried mothers were pariahs. Conventions were far more important than emotions or impulses.

But the old Latin tag about driving out Nature by the

door (she was bound to return by the window) still applied. Behind the cosy domestic scenes of Christmas carols and tartans, of grateful menials and respectful labourers, there was another England, another world. Prostitution was rife, venereal disease accepted as something that every adult male must have caught at one time or other. Lower class women were helpless against the seduction or rape by their masters; at the most they could sell their favours for a modest sum if they did not want to be totally exploited.

As for literature, there has never been such a production of pornography as in these decades. Most of the present purveyors of undiluted obscenity are mining the rich veins of the eighteen-sixties and eighteen-eighties. From *The Pearl* to *The Lustful Turk*, from *Venus in India* to *A Man with a Maid*, the Victorian age must have turned out more sex literature with not a whit of 'socially redeeming' merit than any other period with the possible exception of the Rome of Petronius and the France of the Regency.

All this was not only kept under the counter, but locked away in safes and secret drawers. Treasures, indeed, for they cost a great deal. Only rich people could afford them. The wealthy Victorian gentleman almost invariably had his little collection which he did not share even with his best friends. Occasionally – as the contemporary porn testifies – these books, often lavishly illustrated, were used as aids in seduction (though it has been proved by our contemporary psychologists that pornography rarely has the same stimulating effect on females as it has on males – or perhaps it did not have eighty or ninety years ago; this is not a statement statistically provable). The only differences between the nineteenth century mass-production of pornography and that of our own age were in price and accessibility. In purchasing power, the buyer may have paid ten or fifteen pounds in today's terms for a single volume – while today he can acquire the same for as many shillings. Much of this material was not only obscene but scatological, which made it even more school-boyish and unappetising. All of it was fantasy – about the general accessibility of females who, after a somewhat painful initiation, immediately took to copulation with a most flattering enthusiasm; and about the potency of the male that was sheer wishdream, able to deal with a whole harem-full of women in a single night or to keep one woman continuously engaged for a week in sexual combat.

But the Victorian years produced another kind of literature that deserves re-discovery and rescue. There has been a good deal of argument about the difference between pornography and erotic literature, between the crude and dull preoccupation with the limited vocabulary of four-letter words and copulative positions and the witty and varied presentation of the eternal advance and retreat, combat and truce, meeting and parting of men and women. Very little of this was published in England where it would have been judged just as reprehensible as the most common trash. (The Victorian censor certainly made no differentiation between Maupassant and Crébillon fils, Balzac in his *Contes drôlatiques* mood and the sweaty and anonymous toilers in the pornography-factories). But they flourished in France, Italy, Germany, Austria and Hungary. Most of them were published in magazines and even daily newspapers whose readers were unlikely to be shocked by cuckolded husbands and errant wives, by tales of medieval concupiscence and classic degeneracy. This was a world in which the electric light was still a novelty – Edison had demonstrated his first street-lighting system when Victoria had been more than forty years on the throne – in which the telephone was still used gingerly and the automobile was not much more familiar than the dreams about the flying machine. It was a world in which a man could put a few gold sovereigns into his pocket and travel across Europe without a passport – unless he wished to visit the Russia of the Czars or the Turkey of the Sultans – in which the established order of the things seemed so secure that it could never be changed: it was just getting better every day in every way.

I have chosen a selection of these stories, fairy tales and anecdotes which, I hope, present Victorian wit and erotic fantasy without vulgarity and without the voyeur's heavy breathing. Some are little more than a gentle joke – others a little more substantial. But I hope you will enjoy them as much as you seem to have done the previous selection, the

Edwardian Erotic Fairy Tales. Once again, the authors are all anonymous though one or two, by their style and approach, can be identified. They all share one quality, one attitude: the belief that the game of love is the most delightful of all and that tomorrow can take care of itself as long as you enjoy today.

Paul Tabori
London, June 1971

The Playing Cards

Two ladies sat in the discreetly scented, deliciously warm boudoir. The flames leapt and gambolled in the fire-place and lit up with life-like colour the painted figures of the screen. The ladies were playing cards – the game the English call pinochle and the French *mariage*. Between deals they amused themselves by discussing a divorce suit, the latest and liveliest scandal in town; gradually their conversation became so lively and loud that they did not notice the intimate talk of the cards which they held in their shapely hands.

'This game is a real torment for us,' said the jack-of-hearts. 'My heart trembles and glows under the soft pressure of these beautiful fingers. And in spite of my proudly erect lance, I am unable to thrust home . . . '

'For us German-style cards, this is a shameful business,' the ace-of-hearts agreed. 'They call the game *mariage* – and yet every child knows that in our bachelor community there isn't a single lady. Our kings must form unions, against the laws of nature, with their jacks. The little boy with the golden arrows is shedding bitter tears at my feet. No one can truly enjoy this spectacle – except perhaps the sow disgracing our ace of diamonds.'

'You are quite right,' opined the old Falstaffian ace-of-clubs. 'They consider us highly immoral because our coat-of-arms bears the glandiform acorn. Perhaps there is something to it, after all. But for reasons of health I cannot permit my son, the king of clubs, to waste his manhood in unworthy affairs with his inferiors. This very day I shall send him with a suitably brilliant retinue to Paris, the capital of the French, famous for the loveliest women in the world.

There he shall woo a bride according to his own taste. Perhaps I'll decide to accompany him – in order to help him with his choice.'

The ace-of-clubs kept his word and the young ladies of his realm had to do without him and the most important feature of his coat-of-arms.

In Paris they stayed at the most distinguished hotel as it befitted such important people. There was plenty to entertain the royal visitors and the staff took every care to make them comfortable. The place was full of playing cards and among them – something that would have been impossible in the puritanic land of the Kaiser – several ladies of truly enchanting charms. These ladies showed some curiosity – and modest blushes – as they gazed down upon the German version of clubs. Such features, whatever assets they represented, were never displayed so openly in France. But pretty soon they became used to such obvious masculinity and before long there were quite a few love-games going on. The queen-of-the-hearts was especially taken with the king-of-clubs – and particularly with his proud and self-assured posture.

The ace-of-clubs was happy to watch the development of this flirtation. It might lead to a dynastic union before long – and the ace-of-hearts who had already sealed the alliance with his German cousin in the best Burgundy did not appear to have any objection against such a marriage.

And so, one fine morning, the wedding was celebrated with great pomp and jubilation. All the decks of cards took part in it. It was truly a spectacular event. Six green jacks (in France they would be called spades) opened the wedding procession, with drums rolling; the green princes played the flute; there were several jacks-of-clubs who, instead of swinging their swords, provided a rousing fanfare on trumpets. The diamond-sow grunted harmoniously and the hound, straight from her back, barked happily. All this combined into a wedding march – no Mendelssohn or Richard Wagner had ever composed a more impressive or melodious one.

At last the newly-wed couple was alone. The snowy white nuptial bed was turned down, perfumed with roses and myrtle. Full of burning desire, the royal bridegroom undressed with eager hands the trembling bride, pressing his lips to the velvety skin of her swelling breasts, nibbling greedily at the rosy nipples. But this was only the beginning. In order to establish his conjugal rights and perform his husbandly duties, he sought for the other, even more intimate charms of his consort. But alas and alack! what a strange discovery his eager fumbling opened up! Instead of shapely hips and rounded thighs he found under his young wife's skirts a repetition of the straining, pulsating breasts and the delicate shoulders. From the waist downwards the Queen of Hearts continued as a mirror image of her torso. The enchanting head with its curly hair that rose above from the splendid lines of the neck was lightly swinging down below, though tinted with a deeper blush, on the flower-stalk of the nape. Instead of slim legs covered with the silky down of ripe peaches, instead of aristocratic ankles and tiny feet, there were snow-white arms, a fragile wrist and pertly spread fingers.

The disappointment of the king of clubs was indescribable. Hopelessly his sceptre shrunk and dipped.

He did not hesitate to express his anger, he spoke his mind in no uncertain terms. And as she did not seem to understand his French, he turned to a universal language – and slapped her, hard.

The queen of hearts burst into tears, wringing her hands above both heads and said in an innocent, choking tone:

'What do you mean, Sire? With us in France no man is ever disappointed if he finds *this* under a lady's skirts!'

Harlequin

Have you heard of Dr Miracle? Probably not if you are a woman; for the daughters of Venus acknowledge no better physicians than themselves and no more efficacious cure than love. Men know that the poison of their kisses heals – sometimes it puts an end to all human ills, including the fundamental disease of life. And woman, be her name Lilith or Salome, Delilah or Judith, considers only those truly saved who die of her kisses. But here's the main difference between the ladies, God bless 'em, and the celebrated Dr Miracle. For he took no pride whatsoever in those patients of his who died. And his patients did not die – or he would not have been called Dr Miracle. In his art he surpassed Hippocrates and Cornelius Agrippa, Bombastus Paracelsus and all the famous healers of the world. The universe acknowledged him as the Conqueror of Death – for hadn't he saved his Royal Majesty, the Sun King, and in his august person the whole of humanity, from a grave malady?

What was the secret of his cures? Mysterious pills, concocted at tremendous cost and effort? Wonderful potions, brewed in the dead of night from unspeakable ingredients? The elixir of life? None of these – and yet his cure combined the effects of all of them. It was a universal panacea for it made all troubles and aches vanish . . . This is ridiculous, you may well say – and you start laughing. That's it! That's it exactly! For the wonderful cure of Dr Miracle was nothing but – laughter. The enemy of all misery and pain, of all diseases and even of grim Death – laughter.

The basic principle of Dr Miracle's medical system was the command: 'laugh!' Whatever happens, whatever the silly excuse or occasion – laugh! For laughter, he declared, ensured perfect digestion, dissolved excess bile. The very secret of life was hidden in life. Whoever remained gay throughout morning, noon and night, was certain to live to a hundred and fifty. But serious brooding, grim worry, melancholy contemplation – these were slow poisons, death itself.

But all these, one might object, were theories. No theory could make you laugh, not even that of laughter. How did Dr Miracle effect his cure? What was the beneficial pill his patients had to swallow, that made them laugh so loud and long that they recovered from even the gravest malady?

No chemist prepared it, no apothecary sold it. The cure was a human being, a single man. The amazing, diabolical comedian of the Paris *Comédie Italienne* whom the world only knew as Harlequin.

Those were sad days, believe you me. When the sun disappears, gloom covers the whole globe. In those days the royal face of the Sun King became overcast and Versailles was plunged into the misery of the grave. His Most Christian Majesty was, in his old age, exhausted by the blows of fate and forgot how to smile. The courtiers watched for the slightest expression of amusement or gaiety appearing on the royal face each morning as if waiting for the sunrise – but the sun remained below the horizon. On the contrary, Louis XIV became gloomier and gloomier. They tried everything but without success. The youngest, loveliest and gayest ladies of the court did their utmost to rouse the flagging spirits of their royal master – and, indeed, their lips and their laps, their eyes and their hands had succeeded often in the past – but it was to no avail. One day His Majesty decided to forego even speech – he addressed not a word to anyone at the *levée*, the *souper* or the *coucher*. And as etiquette strictly forbade for anyone to address His Majesty unless he spoke first, this led to a general abandonment of speech . . . Versailles was wrapped in the silence of a cemetery. People walked on tiptoe and the grave-like quiet lay heavily in the glittering chambers. Gradually the whole court began to dress in mourning. And as flowers pine away in the shade, the wittiest courtiers began to slip away from the royal palaces. Many died of melancholy. Panic grew and spread over the country, the fair land of France.

The State Council held a full session and discussed the situation – in whispers. They sent for the Faculty of Medicine of Paris and told the physicians to find urgently some elixir of joy that would restore life to the Sun King – and, with him, to humanity. The doctors debated to and fro. They found nothing new but unearthed a good deal that was old hat. Finally they managed to give the royal malady a name. They declared officially that it came from perfidious Albion and should be called *spleen*. The Paris mob was quick to misunderstand this statement and almost lynched an English milord on his Grand Tour. They accused him of having infected His Most Christian Majesty with the disease and he had great difficulty in escaping. It was at this critical moment that Dr Miracle presented himself to the Medical Faculty of the Sorbonne.

The grimly decorous physicians stared as he walked into the hall. He was a slim little man with a parchment face; he looked like a mummy with a wig. But he entered the place laughing; with loud peals of laughter he placed on the Faculty's table his huge treatise on laughter and its beneficial medical properties. He seemed to split his sides with laughter as he described the logic of his cure, the result of years of arduous work. At first his colleagues were inclined to throw him out as an impudent lunatic – but he laughed even louder and explained that the sounds of merriment were for him not a matter of pleasure but of principle. This, for some reason, seemed to reassure the physicians and they began to pay some attention. And as they became more and more impressed by the learned references and erudite conclusions of Dr Miracle, they began to smile. The miraculous healer's incessant and contagious laughter gradually started them off – until it became a hurricane of ha-ha-has and ho-ho-hos. When the doorkeepers entered in surprise, the most conservative and respectable doctors were rolling helplessly on the floor. They seemed to be eminently sane, too. It was just that Dr Miracle's method had proved a success. His proposition was accepted and the Rector of the Medical Faculty immediately betook himself to the State Council. Guffawing and giggling, he entered the quiet, dimmed hall . . .

Certainly, the great physicians and medical teachers had been won over by the mere theory of cure by laughter. But what about the King?

Dr Miracle had his answer ready. For many years he had investigated the elements of mirth in dozens of countries. He called the attention of the Faculty to the company of the Italian Comedians. Among them there must be one who was the Grand Master of Gaiety, the Magician of Jocundity. The State Council delegated the Chief Court Chamberlain himself to leave for Italy at once – and thus Harlequin came to Paris.

No one who saw him once could ever forget him – nor that fabulous first performance he gave in Paris. The court filled the theatre in funereal silence. Judging by His Majesty's face there was little to hope. The curtain rose and the well-known characters of the *Commedia dell' Arte* appeared. They too, were worried. The motley company passed in parade: Pierrot and Columbine, Scapin, Scaramouche and the grinning Polichinello. They all watched the King. His face remained stony. All seemed to be lost; some were already shedding tears. At this moment Harlequin – or, as he was called by his Italian admirers, Arlecchino – made his entrance. And as if at a magic touch, the whole atmosphere of the theatre changed. They all felt this magnetic touch, this invisible fluid of electrifying humour.

Who was this man of mystery? Whoever he was, he proved a genius of gaiety, a wizard of wit, the very god of laughter. He pranced in his striped costume and the velvet mask on his face expressed a hundred moods, a thousand jests. He had a score of different voices and every one of them set the listeners aflame. He sent forth rockets of sizzling wit, fireworks of comic invention the like of which the world had never seen. At this point there was a restless stirring in the audience. They all wanted to laugh – but dared not. A shiver of terror replaced the overwhelming urge to laughter. Great God, if someone were to guffaw while the King remained sunk in his gloom! They all watched the royal visage anxiously. He was certainly paying attention. He threw back his head – probably alarmed by the fact that anyone could find the spectacle on the stage amusing. Suddenly a nervous twitch rippled over his lips. He seemed to try and control it . . . and that was the moment for which Harlequin had waited. He sent up the rocket of that world-famous joke which I need not repeat – for everybody knows it well enough by now. Then he stepped right up to the footlights, looked straight at Louis XIV and said, daringly:

'Sire, why don't you laugh? Let the sun rise again over France . . .'

And this was the historical moment when the sun *did* rise again over France. Louis the Fourteenth was beaming and he laughed, hearty and loud. For a moment the courtiers hesitated. The Sun King realised that he was laughing alone – so he opened his arms wide in a right royal gesture. And now the storm of mirth burst – but politely, according to the rules of etiquette. The Dauphin laughed first, then Monsieur, then the Princes of the Blood; they were followed by the Contis and the Condés, the royal bastards, the peers, the ordinary dukes and marquesses, right down to the members of the Academy. The Ambassadors present participated in this laughing scale according to the order of their seniority. This was, by the way, the momentous occasion when a dispute of precedence arose between the British and the Russian Ambassador. It was settled, fittingly, by a duel. Only one member of the diplomatic corps did not laugh – an old Spanish grandee whose unrelieved grimness was not only noticed but almost led to diplomatic complications. However, he explained his defection: an unfortunate love affair had caused him to pledge himself never to laugh – and he had kept it for fifty years.

Dr Miracle's system was fully vindicated. The long eclipse had ended and earth awakened to a new glory under the sun that radiated from Versailles.

But, once again, who was this mysterious comedian? He never took off his mask and after each performance he disappeared. No one had seen Harlequin outside the theatre, off the stage. Dr Miracle, naturally, wanted to thank him for his share in his own success – but his fellow troupers would not even tell him his address.

The news of the miraculous royal cure spread like wildfire. The Sun King himself showered favours upon Dr Miracle. He became an important personage, powerful and rich. Encouraged by success, he extended the field of his work and, defying the medical faculty, proclaimed boldly that this cure was a univesal panacea and that no illness could resist it. The blind and the lame flocked from all over the world to Paris. And what did Dr Miracle do to cure them? He took the lot to the performances of the Comédie Italienne. The theatre was practically turned into a hospital. Were they all cured? It would be impossible to say. But Dr Miracle almost beggared all the other doctors of France and boasted that he had restored the health of every ailing person in the whole country.

Did he speak the truth? You might doubt it; but certainly there was *one* patient left whom Dr Miracle's cure of laughter could not help.

It happened on the very day when the great healer planned to announce to His Majesty that there were no more sick people in his entire empire. Before he set out for Versailles, there came an urgent call. He put on his most elaborate wig and entered his carriage. He was driven a long way into the suburbs. There the carriage stopped outside a neglected garden; in the middle of it stood a small, ramshackle house, not much better than a hermit's hut.

Dr Miracle entered, somewhat surprised. There was no trace of any servants—nor any human being at all. He walked through empty rooms; here and there grass had grown through the cracks in the floor. Finally he found a door and stepped through it into the only inhabited chamber in the house.

He stopped just inside, startled. For once his famous laugh was stilled. What den was this, what refuge of a world-weary sage? The walls were lined with books. Alembics and other instruments of alchemy stood on the table. Among the piles of ancient, dusty tomes and mouldy rolls of parchment he saw a narrow bed.

And on that bed lay a man, his face weary, his expression one of despair. His face was ageless; it seemed to have never known a happy smile. Its very wrinkles expressed melancholy. He did not move when the doctor entered but remained staring into emptiness.

'You dwell far from the rest of mankind, monsieur.'

'The farther the better,' replied the grim man.

'Don't you know of our great Paris at your doorstep?'

'I know it well enough. I am not interested.'

'Are you a man of science?'

'What a stupid name for our lack of wisdom! Vanity of vanities!'

'Well then, why do you read all these books?'

'So I can realise the futility of it all even better.'

'What is then your profession?'

'To hate the human race.'

'Have you any complaints? What is your trouble?'

'I'm bored with life. Please help me.'

'Hmmm . . . it looks like an excess of bile. But it's easy enough to cure. All you need is to cheer up.'

'I can't.'

'Really? couldn't you ever laugh – freely, loudly, heartily?'

'No, that's quite impossible.'

'Well, you've sent for the right physician. I'm Dr Miracle, the discoverer of the laughter-cure. It's very simple – yet efficient. I prescribe for you fifteen evenings at the Comédie Italienne. There's my most miraculous pill – Harlequin. If you hear him, see him, you'll be cured . . .'

The man with the weary face bowed his head.

'Have you no other cure to offer?'

'What? But this is the surefire one.'

'Your prescription won't cure me. Harlequin can't help my case.'

'But he helps everybody. Go and see him this very evening.'

'I can't do that, doctor.'

'But why not?'

The hater of the human race turned towards the wall with a bitter groan.

'*Because I am Harlequin.* And the comedy is ended. Good night to you, Dr Miracle.'

Fair Judgement

The moment he saw her shoulders, dazzling white with the butterfly beauty-spot marking the deliciously firm slope dipping towards her decolletage, the Chevalier de Langevin was smitten to the core.

Her dress was the colour of flaming puppies – except at her bosom where an undulating strip of gold held two crystal peepholes. The nipples that looked through them with an innocent and steadfast curiosity were the most delicate pink with just a shade of brown. The hand-held mask was black and the eyes that balanced the roseates were of a translucent green. Beneath it the curve of her red lips was like the soft curve of angel's wings.

The Ball was one of those large inordinately dull affairs which the Marquise de Fenelon gave every time she took a new lover, which was all too often. Raimond de Langevin turned to his best friend, the Comte d'Orpesson, and said, a little hoarsely:

'Who's that vision in purple and gold? I must have her!'

D'Orpesson raised his eyebrows high above his small puce mask.

'That will be difficult.'

'Has she a jealous husband?'

'Not particularly.'

'Is she pious? But incense is a powerful aphrodisiac. If I knew which church she frequents ... '

'She only prays to her own gods.'

'Well, then?'

'That's the Beauty Who Knows No Mercy. She lives in the Rue Vaugirard and her name is Florabelle.'

'A courtesan? I can't believe it.'

'No, not a courtesan. Much, much more, my friend. A lady who values herself so highly that she does not sell her favours – she leases them for as much as it would cost you to provision a division of cavalry.'

'I don't believe it.'

'Find out for yourself. Or ask M. Filon whom she reduced from a rich tax collector to a poor clerk in the War Office. Then there is Lord Aversham whose ancestral acres have shrunk to a kitchen-garden because of Florabelle's appetite. And the Grand Duke Vladimir . . .'

'I don't want to hear any more! I think you're just jealous – see, she's just given me a most dazzling smile!' And he left his friend standing.

But alas, d'Orpesson was telling the truth – if anything, he understated it. For when Raimond de Langevin called – by invitation – at Florabelle's charming little house in the Rue Vaugirard, he was received by a solemn and courteous *major domo*; and he was informed, promptly, that before he could see Madame there was a small formality to be arranged – a deposit of five thousand livres.

'Five thousand livres!' the Chevalier exclaimed. 'Whatever for?'

'For spending half-an-hour in Madame's company. Each subsequent hour is, however, charged at a reduced rate of two thousand livres.'

De Langevin's annual income was three thousand livres – which enabled him to cut a modestly dashing figure at court. He had hoped to spend not half an hour but the whole night with Florabelle. At a rough calculation this would consume his entire revenue for the next ten years.

He tried to bargain, to cajole, to offer a modest bribe – all in vain. The *major domo* remained inflexible, the doors to the boudoir relentlessly locked. And in the end he had to beat an ignominious retreat, cursing the mercenary beauty.

But he still remembered the lips, the nipples, the velvety skin, the green of her eyes. And so he dreamt that night – a delicious, wonderful dream in which he peeled her from her bodice and hoopskirt, from the lacy petticoats and batiste drawers until her rosy nakedness shivered and burned in his arms. It was a most satisfactorily prolonged dream in which his passion was fully and perfectly consummated – and it did not cost him a blessed *sou*.

He was brimming over with happiness and when he ran into his friend, the Comte, under the trees of the Palais Royal, he naturally had to relate to him the delightful and (above all) most economical night he had spent with Florabelle. D'Orpesson laughed and congratulated him. Raimond naturally asked him to keep the matter a secret; and just as naturally the Comte repeated it within an hour to six different people who, in turn, passed it on to their friends. By six o'clock that evening it reached the lovely Florabelle. First she was amused, then flattered and finally became very angry. She sent for Maitre Duplessis, the advocate, and though he demurred at first, insisted that he should institute a law-suit at once – for trespass and theft.

The law moves slowly and it was six months before the learned judge, the Sieur Follain, heard the case.

'There is not the slightest doubt about it,' pleaded Maitre Duplessis eloquently, 'that the defendant trespassed upon the privacy of my client, that he invaded what is her most personal property, to wit, her body. Furthermore this property also represents her capital which she has never spent but preserved by leasing it for definite periods and with full reservation of her rights of ownership. We demand that the Chevalieur de Langevin should be made to pay the full fee my client regularly charges with a proper *amende* for the loss she suffered, not to mention compound interest and costs.'

Florabelle wore her most demure and most provocative dress and the judge examined her with obvious pleasure. The Chevalier was still a little dazed by this unexpected turn of events; acting as his own counsel he declared that after all, it was only a dream – and what greater compliment could a man pay a woman than to dream about her?

The judge heard both parties with exemplary patience, tugged his goatee and then delivered his judgement:

'It is perfectly true that the defendant has committed a serious trespass upon the private property of the plaintiff. This was compounded by the fact that he made his trespass public knowledge. We therefore decree that he should compensate Mademoiselle Florabelle in proper fashion. Let him produce the fifteen thousand livres which she demands in the coin of the realm. Let this be done in the presence of witnesses appointed by the court. Let him count out the money, piece by piece. Let her listen to the clink of the gold and let her dream that she has received full settlement. For as the Chevalier de Langevin wronged her in the world of shadow and sleep, let her compensation be in the same currency and let her pay the costs of this action.'

All Paris thought that this was an eminently fair judgement. All Paris – except Florabelle. But fortunately for her there were plenty of men who wanted more than just dream about her embraces.

The Grateful Stag

This is *not* the story of the stag that carried the cross between its antlers and whose encounter with St Hubertus was so edifying. Nor that of Genoveva's doe. Still, this is a highly moral tale, for it proves once again the gratitude of animals for any kindness received.

A fine twelve-pointer, slightly wounded by a hunter's bow, was pursued by the eager, ruthless pack. In its wild flight it came upon a forest chapel with a small hut next to it. A hermit dwelled here who spent his life in prayer and pious contemplation. He was still a young man yet he had turned away from the sinful world of the flesh.

He had just stepped from the chapel when he caught sight of the bleeding animal, looking at him with deadly fear in its large brown eyes and pleading for a haven.

'Refuge shall not be denied to those in need!' spoke the hermit, full of pity. 'Quick – get into the chapel!'

The stag did not wait for a second invitation; it bounded inside and the heavy oaken portal crashed shut behind him. The pack wanted to follow but the hermit drove them back with a swinging cudgel.

When the hunters arrived, they thought that the rage of the hounds was directed at the pious hermit in his hairen habit and the stick he held high. They did not notice that some of the most furious dogs were jumping again and again at the door of the chapel and then, barking wildly, began to circle the small house of God. They thought that this inexplicable behaviour was due to the strange appearance of the forest-dweller – and they were reluctant to hurt him in any way or offend him because he held the reputation of a holy man. So they called back the hounds, fastened them by their long leashes to their saddles and parted with deep respect from the hermit, continuing the hunt in another part of the forest.

The stag was saved.

When the hermit opened the door of the chapel and let him out, the twelve-pointer was filled with such burning, overwhelming gratitude that he suddenly acquired the ability to put it into human speech.

'Tell me your greatest wish,' it said, turning to its saviour.

The hermit caressed the shining coat of the stag with his left hand while he struck his own chest with his right as he answered:

'No other wish must burn in this heart but to please God and do good for the benefit of the human race.'

This made the stag both sad and puzzled; day and night it brooded how he could show its gratitude to the man who had saved its life.

On a beautiful Sunday morning – the close season had almost reached its end – the stag passed confidently the forester's daughter, a beautiful creature of seventeen summers. In her virginal eyes there was the glimmer of a gentle longing. And when the twelve-pointer saw the lovely maiden, it could not help thinking of the young hermit: 'To please God and do good for the benefit of the human race...' That is my saviour's heartfelt desire, it told itself.

It lowered the magnificent spread of its antlers in front of the delightful girl who nodded in a friendly manner, for she thought this was a tribute paid to her youthful beauty. But the next moment she let out a cry of terror; she felt the ground slipping from under her feet; she had been lifted up and was now hanging, with her skirts all in a tumble, at the top branches of these powerful and towering antlers.

With its head held high, the stag carried its booty through the forest. The birds of the woods still sing of the beauties her posture disclosed; the hedge-roses still blush when they recall them. The stag carried her from the forester's cottage to the hermit's hut and bedded her down on the soft moss.

And those two young people found joy in each other in

the manner of Adam and Eve. But the grateful stag murmured to itself: 'This pleases God and certainly does good to the human race . . . '

For it was a very wise and very practical stag.

The Constant Maiden

The whole wide hillside under the ridge was covered with the vineyards of the Count, our lord. The houses and fields of the valley were his – and so was the town with its towers and squares beyond the mountains. We ploughed his land in the spring, harvested his corn in the summer, picked his grapes in the autumn. In winter we huddled in the cottages and sang the praises of his magnanimous kindness while we spun flax and whittled yokes and clothes pegs in his service.

Those were fine times. The cool, shiny October days echoed with our singing. Our faces were rosy, our eyes bright, our hands clever and our hearts happy. And as if all this hadn't been enough – I found a lover. I was fifteen and he was the son of the Count's head coachman.

It was a fat year – I think not a single belly stayed hungry in our land. I was a child yet hot with love; on this very day I never cooled. Peter was only eighteen himself but he'd reached man's estate; he knew all the things his father did and was even a better coachman than his father. I'd met him first at harvest time and by the time grape-picking began, he was the only reason for my life, warmer than any sun, more nourishing than the finest rye bread; far more my master than the Count we all served. All through the valley it was known that he was my chosen lover; the news was carried to my mother and she wrote me a warning letter.

'*Take care of yourself, Julie,*' she wrote, '*I hear you're keeping company with the son of the head coachman. I don't know the boy but if you've grown to be fond of him, he must be a decent lad; yet I know his father. He is the most famous coachman in the country, the finest horses are in his care and he thinks very highly of himself. He will never let his son marry a poor, landless girl. True, he is only a coachman, he serves our master – but he is a man of property and they say he only respects the Count and no one else. So take care with that boy – however much he might love you, he can never defy his father to whom he owes his life.'*

Mother wrote this letter just when the grape harvest started and sent it to me with one of the villagers. He gave it to me just about noontime – I was sitting in the shade on the stairs of the vinery; and Peter was walking towards me from the castle. The letter was in my hand as I ran to meet him.

'What's that?' he asked at once and took the letter from me. I let him read it and watched his face which was lightly glistening with sweat. His shirt was white, his hair light brown. He was handsome and strong, just like the thorough-bred stallions under his father's care – and just as restless and easily rebelling.

He read the letter and gave it back. I just smiled timidly; I would have liked it better if he hadn't read it.

'So,' he said and put his hand on my shoulder, 'you're still willing to talk to me? Your mother wrote the truth,' and he looked into my face with his bold and bright eyes.

'You know very well that I . . . I don't care about all that,' I said, stammering a little. 'I can even be your servant. If I don't deserve any better!'

Peter sat down on the cool stairs and looked up at me from the shade.

'Think it over,' he said in a little while. 'Any other man would be glad to get a girl like you. You are pretty, you are sweet, you are good – you'll find a man to give you all you deserve.'

'Why do you say that?' I asked violently. 'You know I don't want anybody else and if you don't want me, I'll stay alone.'

His arms went out to me with a smile. He pulled me down, pressed his face to mine and said: 'You see, I want a girl who is nowhere in the world to be found.'

'Tell me what you want me to be like!'

He turned my face in his hand and gave me a long look.

'You ought to know,' he said at last and let me go with another smile. 'The girl who suits me will certainly know. I can't tell her. If I wanted to, I wouldn't know how. Maybe whenever I can love you as much as you love me . . .'

'Can't you now?' I asked, startled.

'Silly goose,' my lover said. 'If I didn't love you as you think I do, I'd never even talk to you. But I don't want to love as others do – as you love yourself, understand? That's all too little for me; that kind of love I don't even need. I'm well-off without it. My father didn't love my mother either. He just married her because she pleased him.'

He gave me a thoughtful look.

'You're a crazy little duck,' he said and gazed towards the valley. 'And I'll be leaving you, sure enough. The Count wants me to ride his race horses – he wants to take me to foreign parts; he says I ought to be with the best jockeys and the best horses. He says I could be the first of the lot.'

'The Count told you that?'

'He sent me word – by my father.'

'And you? Are you going away?'

'I don't know yet,' he said and suddenly he pressed me hard in his arms. 'Shall I go? Or shan't I?'

'Don't go,' I said very quietly. 'Nobody can make a greater man out of you than . . .'

'Than you – is that what you wanted to say?'

'No,' I said in a hard voice. 'A greater man than you are right now. For no one can tell you what to do.'

'What of the Count?'

'The Count? He's like the sky and the stars. He says nothing. He doesn't come down, he doesn't care. Whatever we do, we do for ourselves.'

'All right,' my lover said and got up and lifted me in the air swinging me and laughing at me. 'You'd better go now – the others are up on the hill, working . . .'

He put me down. 'In the evening – if you like – come to the well on the other side of the valley.'

He walked off in his topboots, stepping lightly and I climbed fast among the heavily-laden vines, back to my work.

The days were drawing in; though the autumn was warm it could not stay the sun. Darkness fell early but in the short, golden afternoons our vineyard was like the land of Canaan. A huge, rounded hill gave off the scent of grapes, young wine and peaches; there was the miraculous taste of a rich fall in our mouths and in our bodies the playful strength sun and soil had given us. As if all of us had been born from the mating of violent, most passionate and most gentle lovers.

When darkness came, we sat down to supper, at a long table, in the open. We were our master's guests and he provided good, spicy food and vintage wine. That evening I hurried with my meal and started off across the valley immediately. I wrapped my shawl around me as I walked – it would have been hard to stop on the steep path. Some people, coming from the opposite direction, shouted a teasing jest at me. I just waved at them and hurried past until at last I reached the broad, winding highway at the bottom of the valley. It was cool down here, the trees were half-bare as they shook in the freshening breeze; above me in the veiled sky the stars were barely alight. Soon, I thought, I would be with him, in my lover's arms. I walked in the middle of the road, there was not a soul about, the dairy farm was some distance away and not even the barking dogs could be heard. As I walked along suddenly, as if they had risen from the ground, the Count's four-in-hand appeared in front of me – I was almost struck down by the hooves of the dancing stallions.

But the coachman stopped them in time. They reared and stood still. I stepped back, then turned and was going to pass to the right of the carriage; I thought that if the Count was being driven home, I would drop a curtsey and wish him a peaceful good night. But someone called to me from above – and the voice was familiar:

'Hey you – aren't you my son's wench?'

I had never met Peter's father – but I always thought he must be looking like this man did. He held the reins in one hand and sat up straight in his splendid clothes – just like his son. His hair was grey and so was his moustache and he was sturdy and plump – befitting a man of forty, a person of quality and importance. The carriage was empty. We were alone – he, his four horses and I, standing on the roadside.

'I am,' I said and gazed at his proud face in a daze.

'Well, if you are, come and sit up here beside me. Hurry.'

'I can't,' and I shook my head busily.

'Maybe my son's waiting for you?'

'Yes,' I said softly. 'He is.' And suddenly I glanced around for I badly wanted to get away from him.

'Hey,' he said, 'I told you to get up here on the box. Didn't you hear me?'

'I won't,' I said stubbornly.

'You won't?' He lifted his whip and made it hiss through the air. 'Well, if you won't climb up this very moment, I'll teach you a lesson – like any stubborn filly.'

'Go ahead,' I said and started to tremble in my whole body.

But he didn't – not yet.

'You're the daughter of Aron Tutsek of Gombas?'

'I am.'

'I know your father,' he said with a brief sneer. 'I'll take you home to him . . . ' And he lashed out with the whip so that its thin end curled around my calf.

'Oh!' I said and started to cry violently. But he cracked the whip again. The thin leather strip burned its mark all over my body; my arms, my face, my neck all bore its fiery track.

'Will you get up now?'

'No,' I said and I was now huddled on the ground, next to the heavy wheel. 'I won't.' I wanted to jump up to run away but he got off, gathered me in his arms and plumped me down on the box as if I were a bundle. I closed my eyes, weak with pain and by the time I opened them, we were rushing like the wind along the highway. I was covered in blood, half-fainting, ready to scream at the galloping horses. Beside me, Peter's father was silent.

'Why do you this to me?' I asked, sobbing, as I grabbed his arm. 'Do I harm your son? I'd rather die than do him any hurt.'

'I didn't breed him for you,' he said, without looking at me.

'But why do you keep him from me? What can I do? Peter knows what's right – it shall be all as he wants it.'

'No,' he said. 'But as *I* want it. Peter doesn't know himself yet who he is. I do.'

The four horses, four devils, rushed along the smooth highway, stretching their legs and necks towards the horizon; the trees slipped past, singing in the wind. I closed my eyes again and pulled up my legs a little. I thought I'd jump from the box – and run back to where Peter was waiting for me. But his father must have sensed my purpose for he grabbed my arm with his free hand and it was like an iron vice as he gripped me.

'I'll tell your father to keep you at home. And now keep quiet, you wretched girl!'

Now he looked at me, with a sort of merciless pity, and for a long time we didn't speak. My wounds burned and I couldn't stop crying. It wasn't that he beat me – I didn't mind that. It was Peter's father who'd done it – not just a stranger. It wasn't the whip that hurt but the easy way he could separate me from Peter. Why hadn't I run away the very first moment? Maybe I could have escaped . . . across the fields . . . Tonight they'd take Peter from me. I was certain of that – they were stronger, they had tricked me, put me to shame, dealing with me as if I were a mindless worm; never asking what I wanted, whether I was in pain. I wasn't the first girl to be treated this shabbily – but I had thought I was stronger and cleverer than many others.

It wasn't so, it wasn't true; they were taking Peter from me – what could I do? Nothing. At home my father would beat me again. I wished they'd beat me to death.

I sat silently on the swaying box, crying quietly; and I said to myself: I won't talk any more. What was the use of talking to this man, he was Peter's father; he knew all I could tell him and yet he was acting this way. It was a whole hour before we got home. I was weak and half-swooning; I just sat on the box, staring at my father's house and the people as they hurried out. My mother threw up her hands, startled, my younger brothers and sisters slipped from bed and hurried to the door. My father had just come home from the village; he demanded morosely from Peter's father what he wanted. He didn't even see me at first in the darkness.

'Here's your daughter,' I heard the head coachman say, pointing at me. I was still sitting on the box. 'Keep her at home. I'll pay her wages. Get down,' he told me harshly and was about to climb back on the box. My mother didn't understand any of this – or perhaps she understood too much, for she suddenly began to cry. I stirred somehow – I wanted to get off but I hadn't the strength. If my father found out that I was beaten . . . already he'd started cursing and I was afraid that the two men would get into a fight I'd rather be beaten myself. But my father paid no attention to me – he kept on questioning Peter's father how I came to be on the carriage . . .

'She'll tell you,' he said and got back on the box. He gave me a little push to make me get off. I did at last and walked slowly into the house. 'I did nothing wrong,' I heard his voice from the outside. 'You ought to thank me for bringing her home. True, I gave her a whipping – but she deserved that.'

Three days later I packed my bundle. My mother, who was fidgeting in fear and confusion around me, kept on asking timid questions:

'You going away?'

I nodded.

'Where?'

I couldn't answer that – because the answer would have needed words; and words had left me, flown into the unknown distance. My lips had frozen; no words could pass through them, they were suspended from speech.

'Going back to work for the Count?'

I shook my head and pointed beyond the mountain, towards the city. My mother's eyes brimmed again with terror and pleading; she lifted her small clenched fist to me.

'Why don't you speak . . . for God's sake, have you gone dumb? Have you really lost your speech?'

I gave her a questioning look – my eyes were dazed, confused. Had I lost my mind? Had I really gone dumb? Was this lunacy? Was the darkness of the mad like this? But I felt that if I spoke my heart would stop forever at the first word. No, I couldn't speak. My lips were clamped together heavily; whenever I thought of the words, my flesh quivered and there was a stabbing pain in it. So I couldn't talk! I tied my bundle and put my scarf around my head to cover the long, red mark down my face. To cover it as much as I could.

My mother watched me quietly; only her fingers kneaded the hem of her apron. When I was ready to go and saw her sadness – heaven knows how, probably because I could not bring myself to hurt her any worse – I began to smile, with such a true, bright smile as I had never smiled before. My mother's eyes caught my smile as if it were a golden apple and she pressed it to her heart. She did not smile herself but looked after me, full of trust. It was still early in the morning, a grey, nippy dawn, the mist was still lingering like white smoke in the hollows of the fields. My heels made a hard, determined noise – quite different from the soft, springy sound when I used to go barefoot. I walked straight as if I were made of wood; I walked for five hours and felt no tiredness. It was about noon I got to the city and I went straight to the bureau for domestic servants. There was a man sitting behind a table and I walked up to him.

'You want a place?' he asked at once. He looked quite a gentleman.

I nodded.

'You're lucky; there's a lady, a real great lady who's looking for a maid – but she wants a proper peasant girl. You're from the village, aren't you?'

I nodded again.

'Tell me, girl, can't you talk?'

I shook my head. He looked at me startled, then immediately raised his voice: 'Are you deaf-and-dumb?'

I made him understand that my hearing was all right, my ears just as sharp as his – only I couldn't talk.

'Strange,' he said, giving me a searching look. 'You must be a clever girl. How old are you?'

I held up ten fingers, then five for the second time. He

told me to come back in the afternoon. I undid the knot in my scarf where I had hidden a little money and gave him what I could.

In the afternoon he looked at me slyly and explained: 'I told the lady you were fifteen and had never been in the city before, that you were in good health, clean and looked sensible. But I didn't tell her you were dumb. If I had, maybe she wouldn't want to see you. Yet if she does see you, she might overlook it. Maybe it's even a thing to please her. A dumb maid can neither lie nor gossip . . . ' And he giggled.

Her Ladyship, an elderly, fine-looking woman, measured me with her wise eyes and asked at once: 'Isn't there something wrong with you?'

I pointed to my mouth and tried to smile but didn't succeed. Her Ladyship gave me a strange look and she, too, started to make signs.

'Are you deaf-and-dumb? How d'you expect to do your work?'

At last she understood that I was only dumb. She told me to open my mouth to show that I had a tongue . . . and wasn't suffering from some nasty disease. I opened it, she looked inside.

'But why can't you talk?'

I turned to go. Her Ladyship thought that I was ashamed of my handicap; so she came to me, walking stiffly across the thick carpet and put her hand on my head. 'Don't cry now . . . I won't ask again . . . ' And so she hired me.

She had no cause to regret it. I was given a cot in the servants' bedroom which I shared with the fat cook. My masters were well-to-do elderly people – they had no one to worry about except themselves. Their home was a series of luxurious, solemn, expensively furnished big rooms and it was my job to keep them clean and tidy. This wasn't hard work. Now and then there were guests who moved the chairs about and filled the apartment with the smell of food and tobacco. Next day in an hour or two I restored everything to its proper neatness. There were two of us servants and two in the family. I learned the customs of the household quickly enough and I was less than two months there when I learned other things.

They knew that I was only dumb, not deaf – yet they talked freely in my presence. They soon realised that they could do things to me they couldn't to anybody else. It was my mistress who first took advantage of my helplessness. 'But you are dumb,' she said once and gave me a searching look with a cruel smile. At first I did not understand why she spoke to me this way and listened uneasily. I couldn't see what great difference there was between a dumb and a talking maid. Well, right from the beginning they talked freely in front of me about their most secret and personal affairs, they quarrelled and argued and showed plainly that in reality they did not love one another – that they only played the part of the fond couple for the family and their friends. As I couldn't betray them, as I was dumb, they took no notice of me. I found out that they had no respect for each other – but neither for themselves – and that life hadn't given them much. My mistress – whenever she woke in mid-morning, tired, with blinking old womanish agility – said strange things, half to me, half to herself. Peculiar impudences and sorrows – she cried and laughed at the same time over all things. And I was not deaf who could not hear what she is told; I was only dumb who could not pass it on. I realised that to them I was a bottomless well into which they could throw anything they wanted to vanish from the surface of the earth – it would never come to light again. Often my mistress gave me one of her searching looks. Not as if she had not been certain of my dumbness. At such times she only pondered herself – how many useless things she kept in her mind, how many worthless knick-kacks for which she hadn't found place until now, not knowing where to bury them. Yet she wasn't ashamed – she felt no shame whatever in front of me, only because I couldn't betray her weakness and her frailty to anybody.

Sometimes I thought that this service was just as much part of my duties as cleaning the rooms.

I had to discover more and more about my mistress; every morning she found something with which she could torment me. I was the first whom she met after her night's dreams. I took her her breakfast and her stockings. She lay on her back, with tears streaming from her eyes and sometimes quivered horribly. I couldn't feel sorry for her; her bad mood passed soon enough and again she inflated herself and pretended that she lacked nothing in life. As if all had been well and she would be superior to most. She cried in front of me and looked at me as if I were wiser than she; but once when she was dissatisfied with me after some shopping, she slapped my face hard and felt no shame over it. She was just like any other mistress with her maid – maybe a little better – and of course, unavoidably, other servants learn a good deal of their mistresses. It is understandable, I told myself, that I knew more than most because I could never pass it on.

No, I wouldn't chatter, giggle or gossip with the cook or the chimneysweep. I was created by God to love – to love, to be joyful, to do all for my beloved. These people demanded nothing from me except to sweep their floors, wash and iron their clothes, tidy up after them. Neither did they demand of each other unlimited love; they were cool, suspicious, full of gall, unaffectionate – that is why they told so many lies and did not know themselves what their lives lacked. My mistress and her friends played cards all afternoon in the drawing room and filled each other's heads with trivialities. The master was the same, the cook made bad jokes and giggled when her young man arrived.

Once a young man came, some distant relative of my masters; he looked at me and said: 'So you're the dumb maid?'

And he looked so strange as if he had guessed everything with his clever mind. Yet he said nothing nor did he speak to my mistress about me. He came only that one time; my master did not like him. I could understand that their relations had to remain cool. If the young man had spoken out freely an ugly argument might have arisen.

Why was it that only Peter – yes, and his father, too – dared to speak his mind or their minds . . . whatever was in them? They were not afraid of anybody; they cared nothing for those they did not respect; they were true kings of their fates and very few loved them. I often cried over what Peter had told me; but if he had rather lied, I would never have come to love him. Why should anyone have to lie?

Otherwise I was treated well enough, my wages were good, the work I could cope with. Her Ladyship, in her own way, showed respect to my neatness and industry. Later the master himself deigned to talk to me; one day after lunch when I was sweeping the carpet, he stopped near me and said: 'At least you couldn't ever lie.'

I just gave him a questioning look, then shrugged. Must all people lie who talk? And he, as if he had understood me, laughed out loud.

'What wicked eyes you have . . . you frighten one! Don't you believe that I lied so much – that I lied more than the rest . . .'

For a long while he walked up and down on the carpet, watching me with malicious eyes.

'Would you like to be able to talk?'

I didn't look at him; I kept on sweeping the carpet.

'Oh well,' he said, 'it must be a misery – if someone cannot tell about her pains or her joys. A poor devil you must be. But you see, it's a good thing, too – because your joy and your pain both remain real . . . not like with us . . .'

Thus they kept on talking around me; while I who was always walking among them, remained wrapped in some great silence – as if I stood in a church, all the time, even when coming or going. As if someone always walked with me – someone whose name I did not know. He mostly resembled Peter; maybe it was him and somebody else, too, who also lived in Peter, whom I saw clearest in the image of Peter, whose closeness I felt most strongly at my lover's side.

I had nothing in common with Her Ladyship. She was a stranger to me – just like the whole of her household, her children and her guests. I never understood their lives, however much I saw of them. They were all disillusioned; compared to me they were a happy, voluble gay crowd; I could neither laugh nor speak, yet I would not have changed with them; I would have found the burden they carried unbearable – all that betrayal of those they loved and so many other things. What was my sorrow compared to such a load?

Early in the summer we went to the seashore and only returned in the autumn. During the holidays my mistress's life was no different from that at home – she spent the days with the same sort of acquaintances. The sea was truly beautiful, the flowers, the buildings and all that music unforgettable. I did not know why my mistress came so far; she paid no attention to all the beauty, only to her amusements and all kinds of strangers. I walked a great deal through that fairy landscape; it almost healed me, I'd never forgotten it. There were no fields, no vineyards; but I felt that this, too, was the property of our Count. His was the sea, too; and quiet, peaceful people served him with their labour, whatever their work. Or if not him, then another Count or Prince.

We were again at home, in the familiar place, when once my master asked me:

'Have you had a lover, Julia?'

I pretended to be deaf; I barely heard his words anyhow, the blood sang in my ears. He stepped close to me and stretched out his hand.

'Won't you tell me? Didn't you hear what I asked?'

And he touched my arm. I was holding a tray with delicate china on it. I didn't watch his face, I closed my eyes and suddenly dropped the tray. The china crashed to the parquet floor with a tremendous noise. The master jumped back and I left the room – to pack my bundle again. I took off my maid's uniform and put on my village clothes. Inside there was much screaming; my mistress had heard the noise of breaking china and rushed out to me, looking like a fury.

'Oh you wicked creature, you stupid beast, you . . . '

But the master who followed her, held her back, trying to calm her.

'It was all my fault,' he said in his usual soft and calm voice. 'I tripped and stumbled against her . . . '

But my mistress did not believe him, she went on abusing me – and suddenly she became suspicious, she looked at me and at her husband, she grew red in the face and shouted:

'Why d'you rush to the defence of this little . . . maybe . . . '

Now I lifted my head and, yes, even my mouth opened. She dared to talk like this, she who . . . But I said nothing, I didn't speak; frightened, I wrapped myself ever closer into my silence, into this precious quiet; and I didn't care any longer what she was shouting. I can't even remember what she said. I only know that I went to my small chest of drawers, took out my whole year's wages – it was still there, untouched – and offered it to my mistress so she could take from it the cost of the broken china.

She didn't touch the money; she had calmed down and just stared at me: 'You want to go away? You're going?'

This was already a plea for me to stay and I felt tears in my eyes. Truly, why should I leave? I couldn't believe that anywhere else, in any other household, I would fare better. I couldn't go where Peter was – and why should I go home? I couldn't look at the vineyard where I had once rested in my lover's arms.

So I stayed. The days passed evenly; I knew far too much about them and whatever they did or said, it no longer surprised me. I had lost count of how long I'd served them. In the silence of the nights, with the cook snoring on the other bed, I longed terribly to speak my lover's name. His face shone, his eyes were bright in the darkness. That's how I always saw him – unattainable even in his nearness. If I could call him by his name! But I could not pronounce it – I was afraid, so terrified of the first word I would speak! By the morning there were the sores of fever around my lips, my flesh hurt and my teeth were clenched. I grew thinner, taller; my face became pale. One day I became eighteen and then this was also past.

Then one morning – again, it was autumn – I woke very early as if someone had called my name. It was still dark outside and only the market carts rattled on the cobble-stones. I got up, dressed and looked around in the room. I knew every nail in it; I had slept here for three years. Yet now it seemed as if I had just come into the place, as if I saw everything for the first time. Cook was still asleep, she didn't wake as I moved about softly; there was a heavy, misty night pouring from the direction of the master bed-room, they were all asleep; only I felt that it was morning already; as if I walked in the dawn fields. I felt the air of the sunrise. I smiled, startled, to find myself again in my peasant clothes – wearing the skirt in which I had started out to meet Peter for the last time, which I wore when his father beat me.

I did not pause to think; I stepped into the backyard and opened the gate, carrying my small bundle.

I did not speak for I was alone; but it was the gospel truth that I was no longer dumb.

Had someone called out a greeting to me, I'd have returned it.

I was just like I had been before, Peter's girl and not a dumb servant girl. I looked neither left nor right; my yellow shawl warmed me as it did before. I didn't think of going home – yet I set out along the road that had brought me to the city.

I stopped at the crossroads like a watchman and gazed at the carts rolling into town. There were a good many for it was the weekly market day. I stood outside the customs house, with the telegraph wires singing above my head. The carts trundled past, their drivers sucked at their pipes, gave me grey looks. These were my people.

I stood and watched the carts.

Maybe twenty passed but my love still didn't come. No matter, he would get here later. Maybe he started a little later – maybe he only harnessed the horses when I got up. Maybe he heard my call too late. It was a long way to the crossroads – even the fastest horses would take well over an hour.

At last I saw the two horses, trotting quietly in front of the milk cart. For it was on the milk cart he came. Peter was still just a small blob on the box – like the other drivers. The cans rattled, the horses did not trot any faster, the whip also rested in my true love's hand. Maybe Peter didn't know that I was waiting for him? I did not hurry forward to meet him, I just waited – as if I had only seen him yesterday. My joy was such a happy, peacefully jubilant joy . . . He was now quite close to me, I saw his face. He also glanced at me. He was wearing a hat and a small moustache. And his eyes, as if the sun had risen, were shining bright in the grey dawn.

I stepped into the middle of the road and opened my arms wide. Maybe I wanted to embrace them all – him, the cart, the horses. They were right in front of me and I spoke in a quiet shout, simply, with all my soul, my first word in over three years:

'Peter!'

The horses reared up and I held on, shivering, to the side of the cart. Someone started to curse wildly and I stared, frozen, at the stranger. A moment ago he was my lover; now someone else. He jumped from the box and pulled me roughly aside.

'You stupid goose . . . are you drunk . . . or what?'

He pushed me to the roadside and then drove on. I stumbled a step or two, then sat down on the damp ditch-side. Slowly it became quite light, the drivers threw gay greetings at me. Finally I got up and set out along the highway.

I dragged myself across the bottomless mud and knocked on the door. A tall, fine-looking woman stood in the kitchen. Peter's mother.

I didn't wait for her to ask me; as soon as I greeted her, I added that I was looking for Peter.

'He's gone to town with the milk,' she said. 'He's started today with the milk cart, that's his chore every day.'

My eyes opened wide.

'Didn't the Count take him abroad to ride his race horses?'

She did not answer; she took the soup off the fire. Why should she repeat herself? If Peter drove the milk-cart, it was obvious enough that the Count didn't take him anywhere. I sat down on the chest, took off my shawl, folded it neatly and placed it beside me. She saw all this but still didn't say anything.

'I'll wait for him,' I said and looked at her expectantly.

'That's right,' she said and dished out a plateful of soup for me. 'You'd better eat this now – my husband will be home soon and God knows what'll happen to you.'

She gave me a slice of bread; I took it all into my lap and ate the soup – every drop of it.

Now she sat down too and glanced at me.

'So your speech came back?'

'Yes,' I said, my head bowed. 'It has.'

'Where's your trunk?' she asked. 'Did you take it home?'

'I didn't,' I said, surprised. 'That's all I have,' and I pointed at the small bundle. 'All I took with me to town . . . nothing more.'

'Didn't you say goodbye to them?'

'They were still asleep.'

'I heard you'd a good place in the city . . . and made money, too.'

'That's true,' I said. 'I made some.'

'How much?'

I told her. Now for a long while she asked nothing.

'And why did you come now?' she asked finally; but then she realised I wouldn't answer that and so she fell silent. I couldn't have found a better answer to this question than silence. She laid the table for three. It was warm in the kitchen, it shone with cleanliness and was rich with good smells; it was the kitchen of a good woman, the house of a hard man. So my love was born here and this woman's womb had borne him. It was she who loved him best – next to me.

Tall boots made a sucking noise outside in the mud; it was Peter's father who came in, all wet and grumpy.

'And who's this?' he turned at once towards me. 'It can't be that ugly tadpole of a girl again?'

I got up and showed him my face – so there could be no mistake.

'You dared to come here? Have you no shame, then?'

I shook my head to tell them I hadn't.

'Ah yes, you're dumb, I heard you'd lost your voice since . . . ' and here he gave me a searching look. 'But I'll make you talk! Why did you come – out with it, and then . . . '

He pointed to the door.

I closed my eyes and sat down on the chest again. Yes, it was like sitting on five-inch nails, that's what this house was like. Yet I was here. I waited. But nothing happened; he sat down at the table and I heard him ladling out the soup. I didn't dare to open my eyes.

'Give her some, too,' he said suddenly. 'Maybe she's hungry.'

'I've already given her some,' the woman answered.

'You have? So!'

They finished the soup and later some pie was put on the table. I only knew it from the smell. Now a cart turned into the yard. I sat and sat and waited. There were voices outside; finally someone approached. It was Peter. He turned the knob and came in.

He was exactly the same as I had seen him in the morning. He stopped in the door and looked at me. 'You?'

I reached his side and all that was in me started to stir. Peter could stop me. I stopped, yes, for a moment, but Peter said nothing and I stepped over the threshold. I still looked at Peter and he looked back at me, his face grim; I know he saw me as one of the damned in that moment. All three looked after me, I could hardly bear the burden of their look. I walked a few more steps – but then it was as if a shadow had risen in front of me, something gripped my face and twisted my body. I screamed out loud, loud: 'Peter!'

And Peter came to me and looked into my face.

'What is it?' he asked, angrily, though I didn't know whether it was because of me or because of something else. 'What's happened to you?'

'Look at me,' I begged him. 'Look at me – is my face the same as it used to be?'

'It is,' he said quietly. 'It is the same.'

I thought that maybe I'd die now. I lost my strength and I leaned against Peter, my eyes wide open – to see him as long as I could see. I still don't know why I did not die then – for all I had ever desired came to fulfilment then. But we survived. Every morning Peter drove the milk cart to the city; instead of riding thoroughbreds, he was content with these gentle, heavy-flanked creatures. And I was a peasant woman who had learned how to bear happiness – just as I bore children. Two things only remained: I spoke little for I had learned the value of words; and I never raised my hand to child or beast for I had learned the evil of the whip.

The Mystery of Life

In the days when gunpowder was barely invented and the first books were being printed, there lived a bookworm who avoided life in every manner he could. And as he knew that women were the wellsprings of life and that a female was the most perfect embodiment of the life force, he decided to become a monk. For in those days it was only by hiding under a friar's cowl that one could dive into the utmost depths of knowledge, the river of final wisdom.

But this knowledge and wisdom were hidden in a single chamber of the monastery's library which adjoined the wine cellar. Here stood the fat, calf-bound volumes, grinning with self-satisfaction through their copper clasps and fastenings. Here the bookworm was truly in his element and soon became as thick around his middle as the learned tomes. And the only sharp thing about him – his nose – soon acquired the reddish glint of copper.

One day he found among the calf-bound volumes a delicate little book which in no way resembled anything to do with animals. Rather, it invoked the world of flowers for its ivory covers were tinted as softly as a young rose or a lily whose dewy chalice was mirrored in the nascent dawn. And the title was truly intriguing: THE MYSTERY OF LIFE.

The bookworm stared with bulging eyes at his strange discovery, gazing at it long and pensively as if looking into a deep well. And behold! Under the reddish reflection of his coppery nose the gossamer colour of the cover, like the bloom of a rose, seemed to deepen and darken.

'It is obvious that this book lies most fluently – it blushes as soon as one looks at it,' the bookworm tried a feeble joke on himself.

But it was a serious matter – for the book contained poetry!

At first sight that shouldn't mean very much – for people made verses even before gunpowder was invented and printing presses began to work. (And even today there are poems written that are never printed because their authors lack the proper gumption!) But this was genuine poetry, speaking the true language of Apollo. The very first lines of the first poem resembled dark and velvety petals, covered with dew and reflecting the sky and all its stars. Then followed another; its lines, rolling like long foam-topped breakers offshore, carried a melancholy beat, resembling the soaring of black swans or the deepest shadows of a summer night perfumed with hyacinths. But the third poem was an entirely different sort: witty like the flash of a rapier and sweet like a swelling cherry rich with summer sunshine. This poem enchanted the monk so much that he caught himself pressing his lips to the page – as if the book were the Holy Writ or a breviary. And between the pearls of the verses laughter sounded like a silvery handbell.

On this page there was a bookmark, a black slip marked with seven crosses – like a warning sign to stop for there was danger in proceeding.

Of course the bookworm defied it and went on. Nor did he regret this for the book became more and more wonderful. On the next page there was an utterly marvellous poem, as chaste as freshly-fallen snow. And yet, how warm it was! How noble and gentle its swing, how firm and yet yielding its form! The rhythm resembled the rocking of waves carrying rose-buds upon their white-flecked tips.

There followed more and more beautiful poems – but they became also sultrier and sultrier. Far back in the book there was one with such a rich content, such plastic, rounded beauty that it surpassed all the previous ones. And its meaning was far earthier than that of the others. Its magnificent stanzas rang with a peculiar music – like the song of a flute played by a dying musician or the triumphant outburst of Munchhausen's frozen trumpet which had suddenly thawed.

The penultimate page of the book was uncut. How strange! After all, it was a bound copy! Even stranger was a note by the publisher, with an unmistakable statement: *Only he who bought the book was allowed to cut the page!*

'Nonsense!' thought the bookworm. 'No one can prevent me from peeping a little!' And he pushed his finger along the page to have a look.

It was a very brief song indeed. But already the first lines had a truly startling effect. The monk dropped the book into his lap as if he had been stung by a wasp. And see, his finger was actually swollen! What an exciting, tormenting, provocative poem! Furiously, he tore the page open. The song began with a cry of pain – and ended with a sigh of lust . . .

'I'm redeemed!' breathed the book – and disappeared.

But at the bookworm's feet, her white skin shimmering, her dark hair spread out in a sable halo, lay a beautiful young girl.

'I'm so grateful,' she whispered. 'I can never thank you enough – for you have rescued me from my bondage!'

The bookworm drew her into his arms and as he did so, her slim fingers were already busy with the fastenings of his sackcloth habit. Soon he was rid of it. He no longer needed the garb he had chosen – for he had penetrated deeply enough into the essence of all human knowledge and the mystery of life was fully revealed to his mind, his senses and his body.

The Very Silent Wife

In all the fair land of Provence, so richly blessed by nature, there was no lovelier lady than the Vicomtesse Perdigonne de Puysaurin. Her rounded, slightly plump face could be best compared to a dish of strawberries and cream and you did not have to be a cat to lust for it; more than one nobleman would not have waited to be asked before attempting a bite and a lick. As for her more private charms, covered jealously by kirtle and bodice, the swelling of brocade, silk and velvet proved how firm and shapely they were, breasts and buttocks alike fit for the caress of male hands. And in addition to all these beauties the Vicomtesse Perdigonne de Puysaurin was blessed with a most wonderful perfume – without any artifice whatsoever, she smelled like a lilac-bush in May. Her scent was sweeter and more alluring than that of any flower or tree for it was that of a young and blooming woman. When she walked through a chamber and her skirts swung and swayed, one would fain believe that she hid some incense burner under her gown, filled with all the spices of Araby. And this was true enough even if it was her flesh that was like frankincense and myrrh, the mixture of carnation and musk; and it is certain that such a feminine perfume was not meant to drive away the suitors who were already sufficiently bewitched by the Lady Perdigonne's roguish and lovely face and the firm, rounded curves under her velvet bodice.

That was the cause of the old Vicomte de Puysaurin's deep and constant anxiety when the time approached that would take him away from his wife's side – for he had pledged to follow the pious King Louis on his crusade to the Holy Land. He knew very well that Perdigonne was a most virtuous lady, as faithful as she was beautiful. However hard her admirers pleaded and wooed her, she only had one answer – an uncompromising and final no! That was why she was nicknamed throughout Provence as 'The Lips-That-Say-No.' This should have been sufficient to reassure the most jealous husband. But the old vicomte told himself that the flesh was weak – even when it was firm and shapely; that solitude could be a bad counsellor for a lady of twenty-two, however modest and virtuous; and he could not rid himself of the tormenting thought that the precious incense burner, the fount of such delicious fragrance, might be opened during his absence by some daring lover, driven by the passionate desire to partake at closest proximity of those delights, sweeter than all the spices of Araby.

At the same moment of time there lived in one of the caves of the Alps a witch, reputed to be ten times older than the oldest tree in the surrounding primeval forest. Hunters and charcoal-burners claimed that she was an evil one, always ready to play bad jokes on people; but she was also greedy and hungry for gold so that one could secure her favour for a hundred ducats.

A few days before setting out for the East the Vicomte de Puysaurin visited this witch, thinking to secure the virtue of his wife and the peace of his own mind with her help. Of course, he carried the necessary gold pieces in his saddlebag in order to put her in the proper mood. After he had driven off the four horrible hounds guarding the entrance of the cave and had filled the witch's desiccated hand with the glittering ducats, she told him that she was prepared to show her gratitude to such a generous nobleman.

'But tell me quickly what you wish of me,' she said, 'for I am due on a witches' Sabbath at midnight...'

'The cause that brought me to you,' said the vicomte, 'is simply...'

'Don't shout at me!' interrupted the witch. 'Do you think I'm deaf? I hear best when people speak very softly...'

To tell the truth: the Vicomte de Puysaurin had spoken very loudly because he had been told that the old witch was hard of hearing. Still, it was possible that he had been misled and in order not to anger her, he lowered his voice. But he had hardly spoken a few words when she exclaimed: 'Very well! Very well! You needn't tell me anything more. I understand perfectly what you wish. Closed, you mean? Totally and completely locked?'

'Yes, of course . . . but not so hard that she shouldn't be able . . .'

'But of course . . . stands to reason . . . But still, closed.'

'Yes, from the day of my departure until the day of my return.'

'I can easily oblige you in this matter. It's child's play for me who can take the craters of the most violent volcanoes . . .'

'It is less difficult to lock up the crater of Vesuvius than . . .'

'You're a funny gentleman, you are! But let's not argue. A promise is a promise. It shall be locked – as securely as the Gate of Heaven is locked to a sinner. You can mount your battle horse without a care in the world.'

Then she mounted her broomstick and took off vertically.

The glorious deeds which the Vicomte de Puysaurin performed in the Holy Land belong to history and are not our concern. After two years he returned, safe and sound, to his native land but without a retinue or the fanfare of trumpets. Before he entered his castle, he wanted to find out secretly what had happened in his absence. Clad in a pilgrim's habit, a broad-brimmed hat shading his features, he entered an inn which stood on the main road and in which, as he knew well, the young noblemen of the district were wont to gather before and after a hunt. He also found there several equerries and pages quaffing wine and having gay discourse. One of them said:

'To me it resembles the perfume of lavender with a soupçon of red pepper.'

The second spoke: 'I thought I smelled the sharp odour that rises from a bonfire of rosewood.'

'For me,' opined the third, 'it is like wild honey gathered on the sunny slopes of the Pyrenees.'

'You are all wrong' cried the fourth. 'This fragrance is closest to the branch of an ebony tree upon which a pair of doves has just left the soft warmth of its love nest.'

The pilgrim listened to all this with an unease which he could not quite explain. He approached the drinkers and asked with pretended indifference:

'What is this object which has for each of you a different and yet so beautiful scent?'

The young men began to laugh.

'You must be from very distant parts,' they said, as they clinked their cups, 'if you do not know that we are talking of the incense burner which the Vicomtesse Perdigonne de Puysaurin wears under her kirtle...'

The Vicomte, whom no one recognised in his disguise, found it very hard to suppress his anger and his grief. But he controlled himself; after all, it was possible that the young men were just bragging and chattering in sheer slanderous invention. He left the inn and erred for a long time aimlessly in the district; but he still had other bitter pills to swallow. In a green meadow he found several troubadours lying in the grass, with their lutes around their necks, passing the time in lively conversation.

'...I would swear that it was like the powder of sandal-wood Mary Magdalen used to dust her hair ...' said the youngest singer.

'I am more inclined to believe,' the oldest argued, 'that the fragrance resembled the one King Solomon inhaled when the Queen of Sheba, her dress open in front, knelt at the foot of his throne...'

Horrified, pressing both hands to his ears, the pilgrim rushed away.

He met a group of shepherds, in lively discussion. 'It was the smell of a field of poppies upon which the sun had been shining for a whole week' said one of them and the others nodded in agreement.

The unhappy Vicomte de Puysaurin realised now that the mysterious fragrance of the incense burner had stimulated and delighted a great many noses. Furious and burning with revenge he hurried to his castle.

Lovelier than ever though a little plumper, Perdigonne rushed into his arms and cried:

'Oh, my lord and master! How happy I am to see you

again! First because I can embrace you once more! And
second because after two years total silence, two years of
utter dumbness I have recovered my speech!'

The Vicomte understood it now all. The old witch in the
mountain cave had either misunderstood him – or had played
a joke. She had closed Perigonne's lips so that for two whole
years she could not say 'no!' No wonder that so many
people in the fair land of Provence had become familiar with
the scent of the secret incense burner she wore under her
gown . . .

The Love Fast

The Marquise said no. For the seventeenth time and with the delicate firmness and charming smile that softened her refusal though did not change its essence. It was purely a matter of principle. She was a most enlightened lady who abhorred superstition – except one. She would never, never, never sleep thirteen to a bed. And with equal consistency and high-minded logic she would never bestow her favours upon a man who was in love with her. She liked to keep things in their proper places, neatly pigeonholed. Her shapely body, her generous lips, her broken sighs and cries of lust belonged only to those whose emotions remained uninvolved, whose approach to the game of sex was as cool, rational and impersonal as her own.

Unfortunately the Chevalier either did not know this or did not believe it. For six months he had laid siege to the Marquise's heart and even more intimate organs – without success. For at the very first occasion when he knelt at her small feet and had covered her tiny yet surprisingly strong hands with kisses he had committed the fatal mistake of telling her that he loved her, desperately, mortally and unquenchably. She was taken aback for her would-be bedmates were all familiar with her deep-rooted convictions and unshakable prejudices. 'I'm sorry, Chevalier,' she told him. 'I cannot hold out the slightest hope. It is better if you go now; please, do not come back.'

He went but he came back. At least three times a week he repeated his declaration and though he managed to couch it in new and attractive terms, after a while it became monotonous. He did not seem to understand that she had a perfectly reasonable cause for her attitude. If someone loved her, he would demand constancy – actually expect her to be faithful. A lover would try to fetter her – and the Marquise believed in utter freedom. That's why she had married a man thirty years her senior who wouldn't have dreamt of playing the heavy husband.

Now, for the seventeenth time she said no – and she looked quite angry. The Chevalier rose from his knees, bowed and departed. The Marquise sighed with relief and then, having waited a few seconds, knocked lightly on the door behind which her current paramour was waiting.

That night the Marquise went to a ball at the Duc du Richelieu's. When she came home at three o'clock in the morning, her faithful maid Lolotte received her with the news:

'The Chevalier's here, Madame.'

'Is he? I'll soon send him packing.'

'That will not be easy, Madame. He brought his own bed and he has settled down in your dressing room. He has bolted the door on the inside.'

The Marquise, furious, rushed to the door of the boudoir. She hammered on the door – and almost fell flat on her charming face when it was suddenly opened from the in-side. There was the Chevalier, dressed in a silk robe and a night-cap, confronting her with a grave face.

'What is the meaning of this?' demanded the Marquise. 'How dare you invade my house? What are you doing in my dressing room?'

'Madame, a man has the right to pick the place where he wishes to die.'

'Die? Have you lost your senses?'

'Not yet, ma belle. As you are denying me the only thing worth living for, I have decided to starve to death. Here, as near to you as I shall ever be. I promise you it won't take long. Four or five days at the most . . .'

'Four or five days . . . I shall have you removed instantly . . .'

'I shall fight with every ounce of my strength. And I shall scream at the top of my voice – how you lack even a grain of charity in denying me a corner in which I can perish for the love of you . . . '

The Marquise stormed from the room. Behind her, the key turned in the lock.

For the first day she never went near him though she was only too aware of his proximity. On the second day she sent Lolotte with a cold fowl and a bottle of wine. Lolotte was not admitted. On the third day, by some mysterious grapevine, all Paris had heard of the Chevalier's fast-unto-death. Carriages rolled up to the Marquise's door, everybody wanted to call to get a peek at the martyr of love. In this they were to be disappointed. That night the lower classes demonstrated, rudely and loudly, under the Marquise's window. On the fourth day she took a tray herself to the locked door and lifted the silver covers so that the mouth-watering odours should curl and seep over the threshold, through the small cracks. She also pleaded with him, saying that if he took a morsel for her sake, she would forgive his impossible behaviour and they would part friends. A faint and feeble voice replied from inside that he was past any succour; if she really took pity on him, let him die in peace, her servant and admirer to the very end.

During the fifth night, with all her household asleep, the Marquise, wearing only a thin shift, crept up to that accursed door and whispered:

'Chevalier . . . are you there?'

'Yes, Madame . . . I am still here. Barely.'

'If . . . if you still want it . . . I brought you the food you have asked for all this time. The food of love to end your fast . . . '

The door opened slowly. It was dark inside, with only a single taper illuminating the pretty, brocade-lined room. The Marquise stumbled and was caught in the Chevalier's arms. Her very presence must have revived him for he made a royal feast of her warm and trembling body, a banquet of rich delight.

And in the morning when he gathered his bed and his clothes, he was very careful to fold in them the final crumbs of the loaf of bread, the last morsel of the pâtés, the final drops of the wine that had nourished and succoured him while he had waited for the Marquise to give in.

For the Chevalier had been confident enough – but not too confident to forego a little assurance that he would not really starve.

Monsieur De Balzac's Umbrella

Honoré de Balzac did not possess an umbrella. Not because he was stingy but because of his principles. And so it happened sometimes that his top-hat suffered in the rain and lost some of the eight – or was it nine? – strips of reflected brilliance that all respectable top-hats were expected to have.

One fine day which did not pride itself on remaining fine, the Paris sky clouded over and decided to keep on raining for some considerable time. Balzac happened to be in the Rue Vivienne when the rain started; he was wearing a new suit, an elegantly tailored blue Merino jacket with carefully arranged lines, a Cashmere waistcoat and white striped velveteen trousers; his top hat was also new and, as the year's fashions demand, steep-crowned with a narrow, flat brim. It would have been a great pity to expose such dazzling elegance to the rain but Balzac spied in vain for a cab. In bad weather you could never find one – just as a century earlier you could never find a sedan chair when you needed it most.

Balzac stepped into a doorway and waited. Now and then he gave the sky an irritated look but that made no impression on the heavens. Then his eyes fastened on a window in which a young lady appeared only to vanish again in a moment. The rain continued and Balzac looked once again at the sky. The young lady appeared again at the window; there was no doubt of it, she looked across at Balzac. This little game in which rain, sky, Balzac and the young lady were involved, was repeated and – at least as far as the young lady was concerned – it could not be accidental. Involuntarily, Balzac examined himself; the blue coat was a wonderful fit, the white velveteen of his trousers glowed and he was certain of his top-hat's shine without examining it. He took it for a matter of fact that the young lady knew his identity and thus he hoped for a quick triumph of his personality. He forgot to look at the sky and returned the young lady's glances with the superior art of slowly growing intensity which any expert of the feminine psyche could produce at a moment's notice.

A pretty maid stepped from the house, protected by an umbrella; she carried another one, furled, on her arm. She crossed the street trippingly and stopped in front of Balzac. 'Monsieur,' she began with a curtsey, 'Madame is so bold to offer you an umbrella so that you should not waste your precious time waiting until the rain stops.'

And with this, evidently well-rehearsed sentence, she held out the umbrella.

Balzac, for all his expert knowledge, wasn't quite sure what to do. But even the deepest explorer of the eternally feminine is a man and therefore inclined to interpret things most favourable to his male ego. It is quite clear, he told himself, she wishes to make my acquaintance, sends me the umbrella so that I shall have an excuse to visit her tomorrow – the rest is just a little game. So he took the umbrella, thanked the maid with a friendly word, the lady with a look which she returned with a blush and a slight nod; then, protected from the rain, he left the doorway of the Rue Vivienne not without making a mental note of the number.

The next day brought that gently clouded sky which lends Paris her eternally delicate, rose-grey shimmer. Balzac worked all day with his whole immense power and deep vision; but at half past six he tore himself from his desk, dressed himself carefully in the same triumphant outfit as yesterday and appeared half an hour later at the door in the Rue de Vivienne.

The maid opened the door, curtseyed again and led him into a drawing room finished according to the style which we still identify with the name of Louis Philippe. The warm green of the fabrics was in friendly harmony with the light yellow of the wood; a Persian carpet with a complex pattern covered the floor; there were coloured etchings on the walls depicting the education of Amor.

Soon the lady appeared – even more charming at close distance than glimpsed through the curtain of rain. Under the wide crinoline of her light, flowery muslin dress there peeped forth narrow feet in black shoes; a lace shawl barely covered her bare shoulders; the delicate, pale face was framed by artful ringlets which were curled by the genius of the Norman hairdresser in the Passage Choiseul.

Balzac kissed the willing hand, presented the umbrella with a few words that expressed his thanks and contained a delicate hint that he had given the right interpretation to the lady's kindness. The lady accepted the umbrella and the thanks, blushed in the same promising manner as the day before and said:

'I owe you an explanation . . .'

Balzac wanted to protest; he did not want to spoil the charm of the adventure by a too-hasty denouncement. But the lady insisted.

'I must make a confession – and I'm sure, you, of all men, will understand . . .'

Very well, if she insisted! This method also had its charm and Balzac's principles were far more decided about the use of umbrellas than the confessions of lovely women.

'Yesterday afternoon I . . . I was expecting a friend. A man you know, too. You understand it would have been . . . painful . . . if you had seen him entering my house. As the rain wouldn't stop, I had to use this method to make you leave your observation post . . .'

After this declaration an expert in the feminine psyche could no longer continue the conversation. As Balzac left the house, the clouds had dispersed, the sun was sinking, dull-red, towards the horizon and the shine of his top hat – were eight or nine separate strips of reflected light demanded by fashion? – seemed to have declined sadly, even without the rain . . .

The Lady in the Red Velvet Cowl

In the province of Gascony, a most suitable setting for all kinds of tales because its people are too well-attuned to lies to find the most fabulous story incredible, there lived a noble lady who was both beautiful and amorous. This happened in the days when weasels had no eyes but wore instead at the tip of their tails a precious stone, a sapphire in the morning and a ruby at night, in the times of . . . well, a long time ago. As for the lady's beauty and her loving disposition, these two always go together; for what good is beauty if one isn't in love and what's the sense of being in love if you are not beautiful? The beautiful noble lady, Cécile de Sabran, lived however in a much troubled state of mind and did not cease to shed tears day and night. If I told you that this was in grief over her late husband, you would hardly believe me – and you would be right. No: the cause of her sorrow was the absence of her dearly beloved friend Albin de Sédillac who had set out to fight the infidel two years ago and had not returned. In vain did the bravest knights and the most delightful troubadours pine for her in passion; she would not hear of any of them and only thought of the dear, vanished lover. She remembered his handsome features and proud bearing, his pleasant turn of speech and all the heart-warming and entertaining things he used to tell her while kneeling at her feet on a cushion richly embroidered with silver. And she remembered many other things that were even more delicious and far more intimate. For the noble knight de Sédillac did not spend all the time talking; no, his silent wooing was even more skilful and he used his hands, his lips and his limbs with such skill and ardour that it made Cécile's eyes shine with heavenly pleasure and brought little, broken words of ecstasy to her lips. If someone had told her in such moments: 'Come . . . you are to become a blessed angel in Paradise this very moment . . . ' she would have certainly replied: 'Patience . . . wait a while . . . what's the hurry?' – or, fully occupied with the mysteries of profane love, she wouldn't have answered at all.

After all this happiness so richly and fully enjoyed, she was now immeasurably unhappy. Unable to bear it any longer, she decided to make a pilgrimage to the grotto of St Agnes – hoping that by prayer and pious offerings she would win the return of her beloved. Had she been a peasant woman or a burgher's wife whose skin was unpampered and unsmoothed by the long use of perfumed waters and spiced unguents, she would have certainly doffed a rough, hairen gown to mortify her flesh. But it was the custom in those days that female pilgrims wore only a single garment, without a shift or kirtle underneath. One can well understand that such a delicate lady as Cécile de Sabran was unable to make herself wear such rough material which would have macerated her sensitive white skin. Therefore she had one of her maids who was skilled in such work sew for her a cowl of red velvet which covered her closely from neck to ankle, fitting her body softly and caressingly. Thus she set out – barefoot. Her tiny feet, passing over sand and pebble were so white and dazzling that whole swarms of butterflies fluttered after her, thinking that lilies were being scattered on the road.

There could be hardly a more barren and inhospitable stretch than the one led to the holy grotto. Cécile de Sabran had to walk over sharp stones, between thorns and nettles. The sacred likeness of St Agnes stood among tall, black walls of rock; it was carved from wood which had been once painted though the colours were all but gone. For a saint famed for her compassion, she looked rather ill-tempered and grim. But the lovely pilgrim was not discouraged by the tough journey or the unfriendly appearance of St Agnes whose help she had come to implore. She dropped to her knees and placed an ivory casket as an offering at the foot of the statue – a casket filled with necklaces, rings and precious jewels of every kind. For as the saint was a female one, Cécile was convinced that she must be fond of such geegaws. Then she described her sorrow in such passionate words and shedding such heartfelt tears that St Agnes, though made of wood, was deeply moved by all this. She stretched out her arm in blessing and said:

'Your pious zeal shall not remain unrewarded. You will soon see your heart's friend again.'

'Oh compassionate St Agnes!' whispered Cécile, startled but also delighted.

'However,' continued the saint, 'though I was pure and innocent on earth and shall remain so for all eternity in heaven, I am not unaware that women of your age more often than not yield to strange and reprehensible thoughts. I am sure you did not expect that I would provide you with the opportunity for the abominable sins of the flesh to which you may be too much inclined. That would be a most unseemly miracle for a saint to work. Therefore, as I said, yo shall see your friend again – but under one condition.'

'What condition?' asked Cécile, not without anxiety.

'Listen carefully and you remember, you will suffer the most severe punishment if you do not obey me. This cowl of red velvet in which you are wrapped from neck to ankle, which encloses you as tightly as a scabbard sheaths a sword – you must never take it off in the presence of Albin de Sédillac . . . '

'Oh!' sighed Cécile. 'But . . . I can open it, a little, as if by accident?'

'You must not open it.'

'Can I slip it slowly down my arms?'

'No, no slipping.'

'I understand, Saint Agnes. You would not take it amiss, I suppose, if my heart's friend would use some trick I would fail to notice in time to lift the red cowl skillfully – and higher than necessary?'

'You will prevent him from lifting the cowl even an inch . . . '

Having said this, the saint dropped her arm and remained silent and immobile – just like a piece of carved wood.

The joy of the two lovers at their reunion was indescribable.

They could not have their fill of staring at each other and listening to each other. Cécile asked her lover again and again to recount his heroic exploits which brought him so much glory during the Crusade. What interested her most was the tale of his escape. He was imprisoned in a tower rising to the clouds – from which he got away with the help of a strip of linen no longer than the arm of a newborn baby. The magician who brought him this strip taught him the spell which turned the fabric, without tearing or weakening, into a broad and long piece reaching to the ground. Even so, Cécile admired the daring of Sir Albin with which he lowered himself from the top of the tower during a moonless night and reached safety.

But Albin de Sédillac, as we have said before, was not a man content with mere talk. As soon as the shadows of the evening darkened the tall windows of the chamber, he took his mistress into his arms, embracing her with tender passion; and his passion was only natural for Cécile de Sabran was the loveliest noble lady of Gascogne and the noble knight had fully earned her favours both through the faith he had kept through two long years and his heroic exploits against the paynim. You can imagine his despair and his anger when Cécile told him the price she had to pay to bring him back to her – and how she had become a prisoner of her cowl. And being a deeply religious man, he could not tear this abominable garment to pieces (as he fain would have done) unless he wanted to expose his beloved to the wrath of Heaven ...

The knight's sorrow was great; but no one could tell with any certainty how long this sorrow lasted. It is a fact that a young page who eavesdropped next morning, curiously and enviously, near the door of his mistress, heard no longer any sounds of grief – but rather sighs and soft cries which expressed gratitude and satisfaction without a trace of sorrow or anger.

Two days later, dressed in her fine penitential gown and barefoot again, Cécile de Sabran set out again for the grotto of St Agnes. She had a dream which told her that she had to make this pilgrimage at once and she did not dare to disobey this omen. Humbly she fell upon her knees, facing the wooden statue that was even more forbidding and threatening than ever. It stretched out its arm and declared:

'You have abused my compassionate succour in the most shameless way; trying to deceive me, you fell once again into the cesspool of sin. You have every cause to tremble for your wickedness shall be severely punished.'

'Oh, dear Saint Agnes . . . ' stammered Cécile, still on her knees, 'it is true that I have sinned again – but I did not disobey your commands.'

'What? You did not take off in the presence of your beloved the cowl that encloses you as tightly as a scabbard sheathes a sword?'

'I did not.'

'But you opened it a little . . . here and there . . . ?'

'No, I did not.'

'You slipped it slowly down your arms?'

'I did not let it slip.'

'I understand, abominable sinner! You allowed him to lift it with a cunning trick, perhaps even higher than necessary?'

'He did not lift it at all. Let me tell you the truth, blessed virgin! Albin de Sédillac has mastered the magic spell by which any fabric, be it linen or silk or velvet, can be made as wide and long as anyone desires. He uttered the spell and thus, Saint Agnes, it happened that without disobeying you in the least I . . . '

She did not dare to finish the sentence. Trembling violently, she cast herself down, waiting for the rock-walls to descend upon her and bury her for ever. But nothing like it happened; and as she gradually dared to raise her head, she saw that all around the black stones were covered with flowers of every hue whose open blossoms resembled laughing mouths; the birds in the primeval forest burst into a gay song of jubilation – and when Cécile finally risked a glance at the Saint, she saw that St Agnes looked neither grim nor sullen but was shaking with laughter upon her pedestal, wreathed in roses and ivy – she actually held her sides as if she were being tickled to death.

And Cécile understood then that she was forgiven and that ingenious lovers had no cause to fear the wrath of Heaven.

Typical Case

I seldom invent my stories (the popular novelist said); mostly I find them – in the street, at a party, in the newspapers. Of course, often the ideas are brought to me. Not so long ago a friend wrote me about a divorce case in Toulon. A lawyer's wife had committed adultery with a policeman. There were so many amusing details that I had little to do except change the characters and the setting in order to shape my story for the *Journal*. I turned the lawyer into an architect whom I called Durlet and the policeman was transformed into a postman. Finally I transferred the locale from Toulon to St-Brieuc, the opposite end of France. Three days after the story was published, I was visited by a gentleman who refused to give his name. He was a thin, pale man with thinning hair, a small black beard and glasses. He seemed greatly excited, panting for air; his fingers were tearing at a handkerchief.

'I'm Durand!' he burst out at last and glared at me. 'I'm Durand!'

Durand in France is as common a name as Smith in England or Muller in Germany. I could only say whatever I'd have said to any Durand:

'Enchanted, monsieur.'

But this Durand wasn't satisfied with it. 'What?' he roared. 'You are enchanted to see me – me, Durand, of whom you have published such shameful slanders?'

'I? . . . My dear Monsieur Durand . . . why should I? . . . I don't even know you . . . ' As I didn't know whether my Durand was mad or not, I had to try and calm him.

He laughed bitterly. 'You don't know me! But some scoundrel told you the story! And it's pure invention, miserable gossip! What an idea! My wife and a postman!'

Something began to dawn. 'Are you an architect?'

'Naturally! That's just it – every detail fits. That you called me Durlet instead of Durand only made the thing more transparent...'

'But... has Madame Durand... and the postman...'

Durand stepped closer to my desk and shouted: 'A lie! A wicked lie! Servants' gossip. But someone's passed it on to you and you made use of it for filthy lucre!'

I should have been hurt – but I'm afraid I was rather proud. My little story had succeeded in elevating a special case into a typical one. On the other hand it wasn't a pleasant prospect that tomorrow I might be confronted with a doctor from Nancy whose wife had deceived him with a tax collector. Or a Bordeaux sea-captain whose spouse was too friendly with the sweep. After all, the social possibilities of a triangle were almost unlimited.

'But if it isn't true, I don't see why you're so excited,' I tried to propitiate Durand.

He became even more violent. 'That's just it... it isn't true. But all the details fit. My wife has actually visited the postman as you were told. But I knew of the visit. He was sick and my wife is so kind-hearted... naturally some people have used it for their poisonous gossip... and now, since it's been published in the *Journal*, nobody in St-Brieuc doubts that my wife and the postman... I can't stand it...'

I felt sorry for him. 'I can only give you my solemn assurance that I knew nothing whatsoever about you and your wife until you entered my room today.'

He gave a bitter laugh. 'And you expect me to believe that? No, my friend, you won't get off so easily. You've made me the laughing stock of all St-Brieuc; I insist that you give me the name of the wretch who provided you with this slanderous information. I'm going to sue him, the dirty swine!'

I had a lucky idea. My Toulon friend's letter was still on my desk; I picked up this proof of my innocence and handed it to poor Durand. 'Here, read it! These are the facts I used to write my... I mean, your story...'

Durand glanced hesitatingly at the letter, then he took it

quickly, read it carefully, once, twice, his hands trembling. 'How strange,' he whispered. 'Incredible . . . one could swear . . .'

I had gained the upper hand. 'I hope you'll believe me now. You can see yourself that I couldn't possibly know of you. I wanted to make the actual event and the characters completely unidentifiable; it was just a peculiar coincidence that I invented an architect named Durlet in St-Brieuc in whom you thought to recognise yourself and that the policeman became a postman. You can tell the true facts to everybody. The main thing, after all, is that the case itself . . . I mean . . . that there is nothing between Madame Durand and the postman . . .'

Durand looked at me. Not with the relief I had expected. 'Yes, yes, I've wronged you . . . but who in St-Brieuc would believe me? You know what people are like in a small town. And the details agree in such a strange way . . .'

'But my dear Monsieur Durand, what can I do? I find it painful myself . . .'

Durand considered this for a problem. Finally he rose. 'It isn't enough for me to tell people the truth. You must publish a statement in the *Journal* which explains the whole story . . .'

I was little convinced that this would be effective. 'Don't you think it would be better not to give the matter so much publicity? If it isn't true, people will soon calm down. Even in St-Brieuc there must be other topics of conversation . . .'

But Durand couldn't be shaken. 'No, no, I must have some sort of public reparation. The scandal was too great. You must consider that all St-Brieuc reads the *Journal*; in the last days I couldn't walk a step without feeling the grins and sarcastic looks in my back. And my poor wife . . . ! I beg of you, write a few lines now. They'll believe you. You can't imagine how they devour all you write and I, too, have always enjoyed your stories . . . except the last one, of course.'

It isn't sheer vanity that makes me repeat M. Durand's praise; I think he only flattered me so grossly to persuade me. But after all our public consists mainly of Durands and one must please them. I promised to do as he wished and we parted as good friends. At the door he said: 'I wouldn't ask you for this favour . . . but after all, it concerns my wife. She insisted herself that I should come to see you, poor darling . . .' He glanced at his watch. 'I can still catch my train . . . I'll be back in the evening . . . she'll be delighted . . . these were terrible days. Not that I could have ever doubted her – but the people and the details, the circumstances, they fitted so completely . . .'

It wasn't difficult for me to compose the statement. I had the chance to tell a little about the general technique of story-telling; readers like to peep behind the scenes. At the office of the *Journal* they were much amused by my tale and promised to publish it prominently enough so that all St-Brieuc would immediately see it.

That night I was roused at eleven o'clock. A telegram from St-Brieuc. Ever since I have firmly believed in literary intuition, the prophet-like quality of writers. For the telegram said:

'Statement unnecessary stop my wife eloped with postman stop Durand.'

Full Circle

1

He was born in a slum on the edge of the city, in a backyard. The yard was paved but badly. Slivers of granite, little daggers of brick protruded from the ground and lacerated his naked feet. His whole body was scarred and bruised. His name was Peter. Peter Bony. His father's name was probably something quite different, no one knew of him, least of all himself; but he was a lanky, thin child and his nickname clung to him. That's how new dynasties are born. He looked Slavic, his hair reddish-blond, his eyes blue.

No one cared, no one paid any attention as he grew up. He huddled in the narrow, damp little slum yard; sometimes he escaped to the nearby park and in summertime he spent the days and nights sprawling in the grass, under the bushes.

There he met grimy little girls who sold nauseatingly sweet soft drinks. Once he thumped one of them in the back, knocked her into the grass. That was the start of his spectacular career as a lover – modest but promising.

2

From one of the villages on the perimeter a woman came to town. She arrived at a suburban station and set out on foot for the centre. It was evening. Peter Bony was hiding under a dusty bush of the market place, settling down for the night for he had left his home for ever, when she passed by. The moon was peeping from behind the clouds which looked like slightly off-white lace curtains and Peter Bony happened to notice the woman. She had a soft, undulating walk, firmfleshed, a real peasant with wide and swinging hips. Peter Bony always acted on his impulses; he jumped from the bush and attacked her. The simple village woman was so terrified that she couldn't even scream but the moon fell on Peter's face and she was no longer afraid. She even began to smile, a little coquettishly, perhaps even modestly, because Peter Bony's face was a very eloquent face. And that night she deceived her husband without the slightest sense of guilt and with considerable pleasure.

3

Peter Bony sat in the first class compartment. He was well-dressed and perfectly at ease. Only a few lines of determination remained in his face to mark his humble origins. He looked like the product of Eton and Oxford, his trim moustache, his bored, expressionless face, his Savile Row clothes were in perfect harmony.

There had been fundamental changes; even his name was different. He called himself Peter de Bonival.

Peter de Bonival was quite ready to admit that he owed all this to women. First of all to those grimy little girls selling sof drinks in the park whom he had once thumped in the back and then rolled in the grass and of whom he took the pennies they had earned; he owed it to the peasant woman and all the others whom he conquered, without exception, by offering them his manhood like a drug that made them addicts – as long as he so desired. The women were not ungrateful and Peter de Bonival was travelling first class to Paris when his train stopped at the station of a famous shrine, a celebrated place of pilgrimage. It was a feast day and a beautiful young woman with strangely burning dark eyes got into his compartment.

Peter smiled at her, impudently and brazenly, inspecting her through his monocle. The lady held a small overnight bag with a nine-pronged silver coronet on its front. Peter de Bonival began bluntly:

'My lady ...'

'You know me?' she asked, startled.

'Yes. Your Ladyship has been visiting the shrine . . .'
'Well?'
'You climbed the path to the shrine on your tender and white knees to ask for heavenly grace – and the granting of your dearest wish. I know what that wish is.'
The woman with the burning black eyes blushed crimson and raised her hand:
'No! No! You mustn't . . .'
'You're unhappy, my lady because you have no children and you prayed . . .'
She jumped up in sudden anger but Peter de Bonival smiled so strangely that she suddenly burst out laughing.
'You *are* a strange person! Who are you?'
Peter de Bonival thought he might just as well match the rank of the lady – or at least approach it. So he said: 'Baron de Bonival.'
'Of the Provençal Bonivals?'
'Yes, ma'am.'
She was mollified and even offered her hand to Peter who soon discovered that the lady with the silver coronet was the mistress of great estates, a countess separated from her husband because she was unable to produce an heir. And when their shared journey was over, he was able to tell her:
'Countess, let me assure you that you did not go in vain on your pilgrimage.'

4

On the Lido, wearing a close-fitting black swimming suit, Peter de Bonival met an Italian princess. A week later she invited him to her Florence castle and two weeks later Peter was on first-name terms with half the Italian aristocracy. In the autumn he accompanied her to Monte Carlo to provide support at the roulette tables. The Prince of Monaco invited him to a cruise on his yacht. Because of his Slavic features, his cool blue eyes and reddish-blond hair everybody called him:
'The Prince of the North.'
This was his heyday. In Ostend he already felt a little tired, so he exchanged the Italian Princess for a Russian

one. The exchange was not particularly exciting because he
thought it necessary to gamble just to revitalise his nerves.
The Russian was followed by a German – which was already a sign of decline – and one day Peter de Bonival
realised that there was no woman in his bed.

5

One foggy morning Peter Bony woke up in the park. It was
early spring, a blackbird sang in the tree, the bushes were
budding and Peter Bony was in rags. A girl selling soft
drinks went by. Peter, following the old recipe, was about
to thump her back and roll her in the grass. But he
couldn't. Had he succeeded, he would have found reassur-
ance between her thighs; but he fumbled, the girl slapped
his face and pushed him away:
'Stop it, you old baboon!'
That was the end of Peter de Bonival. It was the end of
Peter Bony, too. He had come full circle. Others made a living out of love and the Prince of the North spent the days
and nights in the grass, dreaming of all he had won, all he
had lost.

Yvette's Secret Vice

She was engaged to be married. She was very beautiful.

A strawberry blonde; plump but with no trace of puppy fat, small, with delightful curves, green-grey eyes of a provoking gentleness, a large mouth, a witty tiptilted nose, her forehead whiter than her cheeks, her hair a rich cascade, a tender nape, a swinging waist, breasts of virginal firmness, a light, velvety laugh – that was the appearance, the sketchy outline if not the whole of Yvette.

Her nose, in particular, had been described as a poem. If we followed the example of our diligently naturalistic novelists we would write three hundred lines about this single feature of her delicate face.

Chapelain and Scudéry would have celebrated in six hundred bad but ambitious verses the tip, the bridge, the nostrils of this nose. But for us it must suffice to say that it was *retroussée*, wittily tiptilted, pointing heavenward – *coelumque tueri*, to introduce a little Latin – and seemed to remain on earth solely to sneer by a barely noticeable quiver at the ghastly multitude of other noses.

All human organs – even the nose – have their fatal needs. Fingers want to touch beautiful or firm things, the tongue wants to enjoy hot or sweet tastes, the eyes seek moving or pleasant images; the ears love the harmony of a poem or the rattling of machine-guns. All senses have a preference for extraordinary experiences. Women who love to eat chocolates do not despise garlic or hot peppers. Why should the nose restrict itself to the perfumes of Araby – or Paris?

Yvette's wedding night had come. The young husband entered the nuptial chamber, feeling terribly nervous as if he had climbed thirty flights of stairs.

Little Yvette waited in her bed, rolled up into a ball of rosy flesh, like a white cat on a silk cushion.

Her groom wore a dressing gown and before he took it off, he switched off the light.

Yvette's pulse began to race.

He approached very softly – and did not touch her.

She listened.

'My darling little angel . . . '

He paused for a moment and Yvette saw in the dim moon-light filtering through the blinds that he had opened his mouth very wide, held it for a second and then closed it again.

'My God!' she thought, 'what a time to yawn!'

But he started afresh:

'My precious, at last the day has come . . . '

Another silence, another gaping at her; the bride felt more and more startled.

'Is this part of the marriage ceremony?' she thought.

He went on: 'The day or rather, I should say the night . . . when . . . ah . . . ah . . . atishoo! . . . At last I'm rid of it!' he said, annoyed. 'For five minutes I've been tormented by this sneeze . . . '

'Oh, that doesn't matter,' she replied with tolerant under-standing.

'Thank you, my adored one! Isn't it . . . isn't it wonderful that we are alone at last . . . that we can make love without . . . ah . . . ah . . . atishoo!'

'You must have caught a cold.'

'No, nothing like that . . . but I don't know what it can be . . . '

He was furious. All the romance, all the poetry had fled. He had become ridiculous – in the very moment that needed such skill, such tact, such delicate know-how; he had become ludicrous in the very critical situation which was to decide the future bliss or the future disappointment of their marriage.

'Go on!' said Yvette.

'To sneeze?'

'Oh no, to speak,' she laughed.

'I'd like to but . . . where did I put my handkerchief?'

He rose angrily from the bedside and began to walk up and down in the room to let the storm of sneezing pass. He silently prayed that it shouldn't last the whole night. But he remembered that he was born on a Friday and was sure that some bad fairy had cast an evil spell over his cradle.

Until now he had been free of all superstition. But such a misfortune befalling someone who had never sinned or even railed against divine providence must have had some cause . . .

When he thought that his nasal passages were free and he no longer felt the irresistible prickling, he went back to the bed.

'Ah, here you are at last!' Yvette said with delightful naivety.

'Yes, my sweetheart! Here I . . . a . . . ah . . . atishoo!'

He jumped to his feet. This was too much! He felt like crying . . . especially as Yvette was laughing.

' . . . I see no cause for merriment,' he said grumpily, his voice oddly distorted.

Yvette held her side which was aching with laughter.

'Don't be annoyed, it isn't your fault,' she said at last.

'I should hope so! . . . I'm not doing it deliberately.'

'Maybe it's because of my snuff-box . . .'

'Your snuff-box? you must be joking!'

He was really furious. Now she was making fun of him!

'Yes, yes,' she went on, giggling and touched his shoulder gingerly. 'My sweet little silver snuffbox under my pillow.'

'Why on earth do you keep it there?'

'To take snuff, of course.'

'What? *you* take snuff?'

Barefoot, in his long nightshirt, he was pacing the room. His hair was tousled, he really looked ludicrous. 'Your mother should have told me that!'

'Why? what difference does it make?'

He felt that his whole marriage had gone on the rocks — even before it was properly launched. And he was determined to put an end to it right there and then.

'What difference? It's a weakness . . . it's a secret vice . . . If I had known . . .'

She sat up in bed and said in a hurt voice:
'You smoke, don't you?'
'That's an entirely different matter ...'
'Oh well, we can always get divorced ...'
'That's right ... But in the meantime ...'
He approached the bed, inserted his hand under the pil-
lows, extracted the snuff-box, wrapped it in a handtowel
and carried it from the bedroom. Yvette did not protest.
After all, there were more important things on a wedding
night than snuff.

Personal Column

Anatole Lavaud, senior partner in the chocolate factory Lavaud & Lemarchand, burst out laughing.

'I must read you something, Julie; listen!'

Julie was reading herself and in any case, she didn't like her husband to read pieces out of the newspaper. But he was a kind man, spring with its unavoidable demands was approaching and so she didn't want to hurt his feelings. 'What is it?' she asked with moderate interest.

'An ad in the personal column – it's really funny.' And he read: 'Lost, March 15th, between 12 and 2 a.m. at Maxim's a lady's handbag with initials J. L. Contents: 500 francs, a lipstick, two letters. Reward: 5,000 francs. Deliver: 83 Rue Dambon.'

'What's so funny about it?' asked Julie.

'You're really naive! A reward of five thousand francs for a bag containing five hundred! Quite evident – this J. L. is a married woman, her husband had given her the handbag on some occasion; he happens to notice that it's lost, he asks his wife, she is embarrassed, for she has a bad conscience and a lover who took her to Maxim's. If she can't produce the bag, she's lost. She turns to her lover and they hit upon the desperate expedient to advertise. It's a very clumsy ad – the husband might happen to read it. Such co-incidences do happen. I don't usually read the personal column – but today I happened to glance at it; and so could the husband of Madame J.L.'

'What a wonderful imagination you have!' smiled Julie Levaud.

'Haven't I? And the story's only beginning. The husband reads the ad. Aha, he says, like all jealous husbands. J. L. –

those are my wife's initials, she lost her bag, so it must be the same. And was she in Maxim's? Wait a moment – March 15th? She told me she wanted to spend the night with her mother who had a heart attack. So that's the kind of attack! And what's the husband going to do?'

'I'm getting curious . . .'

'Very simple. He'll go to 83 Rue Dambon and establish that his wife's lover lives there – probably his best friend. The rest you can imagine – according to the husband's temperament, the lover's or the wife's character. But it won't be a happy ending.'

'*Mon Dieu*,' said Madame Julie anxiously, 'I hope it won't turn into a tragedy!'

'That can hardly be avoided. In such cases even the most patient husband runs amok. He works to give his wife a carefree, pleasant existence, he worries, stays awake half the night. And in the meantime the wife deceives him with some irresponsible ne'er-do-well, some fancy talker who has plenty of time – because others have worked for him. Some scoundrel, living in the usual bachelor's apartment with plenty of cushions, dim lights, exciting pictures . . .'

'Don't get so excited! It's none of your business . . .'

'It's just as much my business as any other husband's! I can sympathise with all of them. I'm sure this one is a decent, honest man who loves his wife and whom she has turned into a laughing-stock. And that's gone on for centuries. It's always the husband who's the butt of the jokes. And the cuckolds fill the theatres, read the divorce cases in the papers – and are the last one to notice that they are involved . . .'

Anatol Lavaud calmed down, kissed his wife's hand and left.

Three minutes later Madame Jeanne Lemarchand, the wife of Anatol's partner, rushed into the house.

'Julie, dear . . . I hid downstairs until your husband left. You must save me – a matter of life and death . . . .'

'Don't exaggerate!' Mme Lavaud protested and made Jeanne sit down on the sofa. Mme Lavaud was about thirty-five, a beautiful blonde of smiling serenity while Madame Lemarchand, dark haired and with a small piquant face, was trembling in excitement.

'My husband knows everything!' she sobbed.

'What does he know?'

'No sense to keep it from you. For three months now I've been Gaston Sandal's mistress. We've been so careful, nobody could suspect anything. Three days ago I let him persuade me, we went to Maxim's in a *séparé* – and then the terrible thing happened . . .'

'What terrible thing?'

'I lost my handbag Gaston had the place searched the very next day – but it's gone. My husband asked yesterday about the bag, I was confused, made some excuse but he became wild and insisted that I produce the bag by tonight. That's when I had the unhappy idea of advertising . . .'

'And your husband read it?'

'Yes – imagine! He never reads the personal column. There was a terrible scene, he wanted to go immediately to the address I had given. And that's where Gaston lives! I almost lost my mind – and I did something terrible . . . you'll never forgive me . . .'

'What is there to forgive?'

'I told my husband that the bag is yours and that you and Gaston . . .'

'You . . . told him . . . that?'

'Yes. It was wrong, I know . . . but I was so desperate. You don't really know my husband, he'd have killed Gaston . . . and after all, it was only natural that I thought of you . . .'

'Natural?'

'Of course! Your initials are the same as mine. J. L. could just as well stand for Julie Lavaud as for Jeanne Lemarchand.'

Mme Lavaud didn't think this a matter-of-course. But Jeanne was shaken by a crying fit and it wasn't easy to calm her down.

'You have done a very bad thing,' said Julie seriously. 'You've put my reputation in jeopardy. And your husband believed you so easily?'

'That's the worst! No one would believe such a thing about you!'

Mme Julie wasn't quite sure whether this was meant as a

compliment or an insult. But Jeanne meant neither.

'He demands proof!'

'Proof?'

'Yes. He's going to keep the house in the Rue Dambon under observation all afternoon. If he sees you going in, he's going to believe me. Not otherwise.'

Julie got up.

'This is really too much ...'

Another flood of tears.

'He'll keep it a dead secret ... Your husband isn't jealous ... And maybe you'll save two lives ...'

Madame Julie pondered the problem.

'On one condition.'

'Anything! If only you save me ...'

'You must break off your affair with Gaston!'

Jeannie Lemarchand heaved a great sigh of relief.

'If that's all ... we've had a terrible row anyhow over this awful business ...'

*

'I'm really sorry for poor Lavaud,' said M Lemarchand that night, after he had succeeded in obtaining the forgiveness of his wife whose virtue he had dared to suspect, 'but he is a born cuckold. Nothing like this can ever happen to me, I keep my eyes open ...'

'... and torment your poor, faithful little wife with your ugly jealousy just because she's mislaid an old, shabby bag ...'

*

At the same time, in the bachelor apartment at 83 Rue Dambon, Gaston Sandal found it much harder to win the forgiveness of Julie Lavaud. For it wasn't the first time that she had caught him in such an escapade; while she, during their affair which had now lasted several years, had been completely faithful to her lover.

*

Again, at the same time, Pierre Blanc, a *fiacre* driver,

crashed his fist down on the table where the 'Paris Soir' was opened on the page of the personal column. Then he hit his own forehead. For Madame Jeanne Lemarchand had left her handbag not at Maxim's but in his cab. Pierre simply pocketed the five hundred francs and threw the bag with the lipstick and the two letters into the Seine.

Lucky Man

Paul Königstein put on his smoking jacket, pinned a pink carnation to his lapel, then summoned Walter, his man-servant and said to him:

'Take a cab to the Kaiserhof. Ask for the Very Reverend Florian Königstein, my uncle. I think his room number is twenty-six. Give him my kind regards and apologies; tell him that I regret infinitely but we cannot spend the evening together as I have been suddenly called to Hamburg on official business. I'll be back tomorrow at lunchtime and delighted to see him . . . After you have delivered the message, you can take the night off.'

Walter wasted no time to take advantage of his master's generosity. He departed within thirty seconds and Paul Königstein walked into the large living room of his bachelor apartment.

In front of the fireplace there was a table laid for two. There were lilies-of-the-valley in slender vases and a couple of old silver candlesticks. On certain occasions Paul Königstein preferred candlelight to the vulgarity of gas-light; it was much more intimate and flattering to feminine beauty. On the sideboard a cold supper had been laid out: a cock lobster, a fair-sized turkey, fried to a crisp brown, a game-pie, some French salad, fruit and lots of petits fours. Another table bore the spirit lamp waiting to be lit under the coffee-maker, an assortment of drinks and boxes of cigars and Turkish cigarettes. Two bottles of champagne were nestling in the cooler.

Paul Königstein lit the candles and straightened the small red shades. The huge mirror began to shine, a gentle shimmer was cast upon the carpets; the whole place was most friendly and hospitable. There was a slight smell of tobacco, so Paul sprinkled a little eau-de-Cologne around the room.

Ten minutes to eight . . . Paul began to walk up and down. And now the front-door bell went. What punctuality! The darling must have been really eager for . . . He hurried down the hall and opened the door. It was the boy from the laundry.

'Sorry, Mr Königstein. We got a bit behind today with deliveries . . . '

Somehow he got rid of the creature, tipping him much too generously. Then he resumed his vigil. He stayed in the hall, leaning against the doorjamb, listening intently.

Now! There was a soft sound out there . . . light steps, the susurration of skirts . . . Paul's heart began to race. He opened the door a crack and saw a big picture hat and a white fur coat appearing at the head of the stairs. He suddenly opened the door completely – and stared at a lady who was a total stranger. They gazed at each other, startled; then she walked on, down the long corridor.

He had to wait another half an hour. This was really an outrage! He smoked three cigarettes and gargled three times. The bell! . . . A boy with a telegram. Königstein tore it open nervously. Some friends of his, in Heidelberg, getting drunk on beer, sending him maudlin greetings . . .

A cab stopped outside the house. Yes, it must be . . . of course, she wouldn't come except by a four-wheeler . . . Soon the bell went – its very tone betrayed a small, trembling hand . . .

Paul opened the door and froze. A tall, plump grey-haired gentleman in clerical garb was smiling at him.

'How nice to see you, Paul! It's been more than a year, hasn't it?'

It was the Very Reverend Florian Königstein, his uncle.

'Didn't Walter give you my message?'

'He couldn't have. I'm coming straight from Potsdam – I spent the afternoon there. But you can tell me yourself, whatever it was.'

And this terrible man of God slipped off his overcoat and walked into the living room as if it were the most natural thing in the world. If I shouted 'fire!' and started to run, would he run with me? pondered Königstein. Or perhaps I could drop on the carpet and start moaning . . . would he believe me that I was mortally ill?

Prebendary Florian looked at the table with a smile. He folded his plump white hands and said, genuinely moved:

'That's really nice of you . . . supper all ready. And a cold collation, too! I had a very stuffy lunch with the Bishop . . . I'll enjoy this, I'm sure.'

He examined the sideboard with the expert's glance. He knocked with the tip of his index finger against the ruddy armour of the lobster and grinned at the crisp turkey.

'If I told him that I was expecting someone else to supper?' brooded the young man. 'Perhaps the Foreign Secretary himself. A confidential conference – discussing my promotion?'

Florian Königstein examined the bottles; one of the champagne magnums he lifted from the cooler and read its label. Then he clapped his nephew on the shoulder.

'I must say, you Berliners know how to live!'

Paul made a protesting gesture, full of bitterness. He sighed.

'Oh well,' his uncle said, 'I know that you're a moderate and thrifty man and are only spending for my sake . . . I appreciate your hospitality even more, believe me!'

He sat down, spread his napkin, poured out a glass of white wine and added: 'Well, come along now!'

This was getting serious. Paul Königstein glanced at the wall opposite. He had a fine collection of old weapons; among them, a spiky mace. If I suddenly went mad, he told himself, and killed my beloved uncle . . . I could hide the body in my cabin trunk and no one would look for him before tomorrow . . .

But he did not reach for the mace. He reached for the lobster and placed it on the table with a heart-rending yet inaudible moan. He ate little himself; but The Very Reverend Father displayed an excellent appetite and did not leave much of the huge crustacean. This gave him a good appetite and he made short shift of the game-pie. He began to carve the turkey with considerable expert knowledge when the front door bell went – one short, one long ring, like an exclamation mark. The two men glanced at each other. Paul rushed into the hall. There were soft noises, whispers; then the door closed again . . . Heart-broken, Paul Königstein returned. Down in the street the door of a hansom clammed, a whip cracked and . . . everything was finished!

'Who was it?' asked the kindly prelate while he poured a little more vinegar into the salad bowl.

'It's the office . . . an urgent dispatch . . .' said Paul, closing his eyes for a moment.

'Won't they give you any rest, even at night?' his uncle demanded indignantly. 'Well, you can't shirk your duty. Go on – I'll wait for you here . . . maybe take a nap . . .'

With the stealthy movement of the assassin, Paul reached for the carving knife. But then he put it down again and said wearily: 'No, it wasn't so terribly important . . . it can wait until tomorrow.'

'Let's try the champagne,' suggested Florian Königstein. 'I like a good Rhenish better myself but if you've spent all this money for my sake . . .'

They finished a bottle. Then Paul lit the spirit lamp to make coffee. It didn't matter now. Nothing did.

'Now, this was really a good dinner!' said his uncle.

Outside the bell shrilled again . . . Dammit, wasn't there an end to it? It was a long, ominous ring. Paul Königstein went into the hall, carrying his napkin, a cigar in his mouth.

As he opened the door, he stepped back. He faced a pale, bearded man in a dark overcoat with a fur collar. The late visitor entred quickly and spoke in a rapid, hoarse voice: 'You didn't expect me, did you?'

'Marcus! What on earth . . .'

The bearded man's face twisted in rage. He stood there, ready to pounce, like a leopard.

'Enough of the comedy!' he said. 'I know everything – she's here! You have already defiled her, I am sure. In that room!'

He rushed inside, without removing his hat. Paul followed him. He risked a grin which Marcus couldn't see.

'Dear Uncle Florian,' he said, 'let me introduce a dear old friend of mine whom you must know by reputation. Marcus Ansbacher, physician to the Empress and her daughters. My uncle, the Very Reverend Prebendary Florian Königstein. Marcus must have had some bad news, he looks so excited . . . but after all, we're old friends. Sit down, Marcus, tell us all about it . . .'

The bearded man took off his hat. He was embarrassed.

'Yes . . . it was very unpleasant . . . ' he murmured. 'A mistake . . . a bad mistake . . . '

His eyes were swivelling unsteadily. But Paul had suddenly become very gay. He sparkled with amiable wit.

'Have a drink, Marcus . . . it's really good, this champagne. You too, uncle. See, we two old bachelors had a quiet convivial evening . . . I've always been fond of Uncle Florian . . . pity I see him so seldom these days . . . A toast to Uncle Florian! God bless you!'

The old gentleman was deeply moved by the warmth of feeling in his nephew's words. He rose to his feet and delivered a speech almost up to his best sermons. He was an eloquent man at any time and now he surpassed himself.

Gradually the bearded man's face brightened. It seemed that he had rid himself of a heavy burden and found life now beautiful and enjoyable.

He slipped his drink quietly but then he had to open his heart to his companions.

'You go on learning to the end of your days. I've certainly had a valuable lesson today! One should never doubt those one loves . . . I did you a grave injustice today, Paul . . . and someone else, too. I confess freely that I've done evil. You'll never know what it was but if you really like me, give me your hand and . . . '

'Give him your hand, Paul!' commanded the Prebendary.

The guests stayed till midnight. For part of the way, Marcus walked with Paul's uncle.

'He's really a wonderful young man, our Paul,' the old gentleman said. 'Full of kindness and generosity – how rare today!'

'He has a heart of gold,' the bearded man declared firmly. 'We know it best – my wife and myself . . . '

'You're married, then?' asked the clergyman.

'Four years now. Like Horace, I can say that the gods love me for they've given me a good wife and a good friend . . .

My wife's such a noble soul . . . tonight, for instance, she's at the bedside of a sick friend . . . '

The two men parted at the next corner. And Paul Königstein, alone in his apartment, began to realise what a lucky man he was. And he reflected how easy it would be now to get pretty Caroline Ansbacher to bed . . . with her jealous husband never again daring to doubt her! A pleasure deferred might be a pleasure doubled, he thought, and finished the champagne.

The Extraordinary Wedding Night

'But my darling,' said Mynheer van Crouten who was a most respectable art dealer and lived at the equally respectable city of The Hague, 'don't you think that we ought to go to Genoveva's wedding?'

Mevrouw van Crouten reflected for a moment before replying:

'I don't very much like to leave the house for several days.'

And she added, significantly:

'I am always certain that when we are away, Mietje and her paramour sleep in our bed. And not only sleep,' she added with a sigh.

Van Crouten's face twisted in a grimace of disgust. He was a model husband and very much attached to his home – where he enjoyed the embraces of both his wife and of Mietje, the plump and appetising maid. He was equally jealous of both; and he had equal right to be.

'What makes you think this, Adrienne?' he demanded, frowning.

'I have my reasons to believe that this is a fact – and I have equally good reasons not to disclose them to you, my dear.'

'Still, Genoveva is our god-daughter,' Mynheer van Crouten continued after a brief but pregnant silence. 'We're certain to hurt the feelings of the whole family if we stay away from her wedding. We'd have to stay at least two days in that boring little town and that attracts me as litle as it does you, my sweet. However, one has certain duties of kinship one cannot ignore.'

'Very well, my dear, let us go to the wedding. If you like,

I'll leave the day before you as I know you're busy at the gallery. For as you know Genoveva lost her mother when she was quite young and it is my task to provide her with some advice on the eve of the ordeal she is about to undergo.'

'Ordeal? I must say your choice of expressions and your tone are not exactly flattering for me. However, by all means enlighten the child . . . '

'Poor little girl!' murmured the lady without paying much attention to her husband's plaintive remark.

As they agreed, Mevrouw van Crouten set out next morning and her husband only followed her in the late afternoon. Not because he had to apply himself to the business of his gallery where he had very capable assistants who could sell a fake Frans Hals or a spurious Tenniel with almost the same zest and fluency as he could himself. No, the confidential information his wife had imparted, bothered him considerably and he was burning with a blind fury against Mietje that soon developed into determined plans of revenge. Why, that little bitch had the impudence of deceiving him in his own conjugal bed! Well, he would show her! Indeed, he would show her with a vengeance!'

As soon as his wife left the house, Mynheer van Crouten betook himself to a fireworks maker and acquired a good many explosive devices which he had wrapped up and carried off under his voluminous ulster. After which he sent the perfidious Mietje on an errand so that he could be alone in the house; then he locked himself in the pleasant though somewhat old-fashioned room where he and his wife took their repose. If someone had been able to watch the worthy art-dealer through the window, such a person would have hardly been able to suppress a cry of surprise. On his knees, having discarded his jacket, Mynheer van Crouten was busy constructing an infernal machine, linking the springs of the mattress to a complex system of petards and squibs, rockets and Catherine wheels, combined into a veritable inflammable network whose final result would have delighted any Frenchman on Bastille Day or any British youngster on Guy Fawkes' Night. All this was hidden behind a chest of drawers which he had pulled out from the wall and which hid perfectly these strange preparations. A properly strong pressure on the apparatus under the mattress would produce a spark which, in turn, would light the fuse and produce a magnificent display, both visual and aural.

Having prepared this trap, Mynheer van Crouten was ready to leave. He took a front-door key without saying anything – except to tell Mietje with a perfectly hypocritical friendless to be a good girl while he was away.

Two hours later he arrived at the home of the Van Pouffen family of which Genoveva was the brightest jewel. No one could deny that the young bride-to-be was in every way an enchanting creature. It would be difficult to decide from which angle she offered the more delightful curves. Some would vote for the posterior, others for the front view; but this, after all, was less important than the undeniable existence of her budding charms. She was a blonde with a few darker glints in her hair that made her even more attractive. Young Major van Peten – whose given name was Claudius – was certainly to be envied for the privilege of plucking this peerless pearl, unveiling this inviolate treasure, exploring this exquisite mystery of feminine innocence. Alas, it was vain to hope that he might need some aid in this perilous and difficult enterprise! Certainly, one was tempted to recall the Flemish proverb which runs: 'Often one needs someone smaller than oneself!' The Major was a handsome man; but then, I am not such a puny fellow myself!

The bells had been ringing clamorously, frightening the storks from their rooftop nests so that their huge rosy wings flapped against the sky; the echoes of the tintinnabulation did not die away for minutes. The happy couple walked with beaming faces under the arch of the shining swords of Major van Peten's fellow-officers. The steaming dishes of the wedding banquet presented a sumptuous array and the appetising smells mingled agreeably with the scent of the flowers and the perfume of the ladies. Wines had been flowing like water, glasses clinked. Words passed from mouth to mouth, often slyly spicy and smutty as it is the custom on such joyous occasions. There was even some singing in honour of the newly-weds. Genoveva looked ravishing in her white wedding dress but her piquant face clearly showed her uneasiness, her colour came and went, now blushing, now paling, like the sky on April mornings when it looks as if pink and white rose petals drifted across it.

Mevrouw van Crouten had conscientiously carried out her task of enlightenment and initiation, delivering the little introductory lecture without which, it seems, girls can never become mothers – a general supposition which appears to me utterly absurd. For I know that a great many children are made without anybody bothering about such preliminaries. But whatever the truth about *that*, Mevrow van Crouten's final explanations were beyond doubt frightening and full of obscure warnings. For the poor young bride looked at the same time as if she hadn't understood anything at all of what she had been told and yet she was telling herself: 'It seems that I must be prepared for everything and anything . . .'

This feeling of anxiety and distress was clearly mirrored in Genoveva's face – while Major van Peten who looked as if he knew far better what was expected of him, took on the airs of an insufferable conqueror. This showed that he was lamentably lacking in tact. For a little pretended uneasiness and some compassion for the present state of mind of his wife would have been surely in better taste.

Like always, it had been decided that the young couple would set out at once on their honeymoon. They were to pass their wedding night at The Hague – that crucial night which Genoveva felt closing in on her, as the shadows lengthened and were tinted blood-red by the rays of the setting sun – a night whose terrors increased every moment. When they were about to leave, Mevrouw van Crouten took the Major aside.

'Are you going to sleep at the hotel tonight?' she asked.

'Certainly, coz,' replied the Major with gracious familiarity.

'That will cost you a packet,' continued the thrifty wife of the art dealer.

'Indubitably,' replied Van Peten who also believed in saving a gulden wherever it was possible.

'I have an idea,' Mevrouw van Crouten smiled. 'What

if I gave you the key of our house which I found in my husband's pocket? I won't tell him anything, of course. We are not returning until the day after tomorrow ourselves. You'll be far more at home in our place and you can also check on our maid who needs some supervision . . . '

'You are right, dear lady – it would be perfect.'

'Very well, that's settled then. I'll give you the key in a moment. But – not a word to Mynheer van Crouten; he needn't know anything . . . '

As you can see, both Van Croutens had a penchant for secrets. For the husband hadn't told his lady a word about the elaborate trick he planned to play on the sinful Mietje. They both were used to keeping their counsel – believing that what you didn't know couldn't hurt you. Or could it?

At last – for their engagement had lasted almost two years – Major van Peten carried his blushing bride over the threshold of the nuptial chamber which was the conjugal bedroom of the Van Croutens. And there he watched, in spite of her protests, the preperations of his lovely Genoveva; saw the transparent batiste nightgown shimmer rosily as her young and shapely flesh strained against it; then, a few moments later, with slightly trembling fingers, freed the firm, lovely breasts from their gossamer sheath, tracing the curve from bosom to flank, touching his burning lips to the purpling nipples. Genoveva closed her eyes and was shivering, half in terror, half in anticipation. The major had discarded his own encumbrance of clothes and now, with the practised and sinuous movement of the professional seducer, he slipped into the capacious bed. He was far too experienced to hurry matters but after ten minutes that were far from as terrifying as Mevrouw van Crouten made Genoveva believe, he was ready to achieve the consummation that was, after all, the prime purpose of a wedding night.

At the very moment when pain and pleasure, amazement and delight mingled inextricably in Genoveva's body and mind, the whole room seemed to explode in flashing colour and ecstatic sound around them. Bright circles whirled, stars rocketed, bangs and splutters, detonations and plops, crackles and plops, pings and clicks accompanied the pyrotechnic display that seemed to go on for ever.

Claudius, deadly pale, still fused with his lovely bride, was on the point of fainting. He had lifted himself by his elbows and was trembling violently.

But Genoveva – why, Genoveva, having reached for the first time in her life the summit of joy, ravished and enchanted, blissful in her new-found joy, murmured in a voice full of tenderness and gratitude:

'Oh, my darling – will it be always like this?'

An Apple of Honour

I was born in Bradford, Yorkshire. My wife Yvonne was born in Arles, France. We are the living embodiment of Franco-British friendship – as long as we live in Bradford where Yvonne is a model housewife, the mother of our two admirable children and, except for her accent and an addiction to the kind of underwear which luckily no one but I have an opportunity of seeing, a perfectly assimilated subject of our beloved Queen Victoria.

But when we go to France – and sometimes this is unavoidable for my profession is to import wine and brandy – all this changes. Yvonne becomes a full-blooded Frenchwoman again. And this means that she is an incurable romantic, with an insatiable appetite for the frivolous novels of M. Dumas and M. Eugene Sue. I disapprove, of course; but I must admit that I am excessively fond of her and therefore I indulge her, as much as my not inconsiderable means permit. She does not abuse this generosity, I must concede but sometimes she does strain it a bit.

Like the other day when we walked down the Rue Vaugirard in the rain. We came to the crossing where the municipality, in its infinite wisdom, had removed a row of paving stones and had forgotten to replace them through several weeks. It was very muddy, that spot. Yvonne lifted her head, with her pretty russet chignon, proud like a queen and said:

'I want a carpet, Jacques.'

In Paris she always called me 'Jacques'; In Bradford I insisted on James.

'My dear,' I told her, 'this is Sunday. As you know, the

shops are closed. And we have enough carpets in our modest but comfortable home.'

'Idiot of a man,' she said, quite disrespectfully and stamped her pretty foot. 'I mean a carpet, here. I cannot step into the dirt, can I?'

'But how can I get you ...'

'What's wrong with your coat?' she asked and stamped her foot again so that some water splashed into my eyes.

'But my dear, this coat cost me three pounds and eleven shillings. You do not expect me ...'

'Bah!' she sneered and she could sneer very beautifully. 'Did Sir Drake, the great English admiral stop to consider whether his cloak was too precious when he put it in the mud for *la Reine* Elizabeth?'

'It wasn't Drake, it was Raleigh,' said I. 'And you are *not* Queen Elizabeth.'

Thereupon she lifted up her pretty nose which was in any case a tiptilted one and refused to speak to me for quite five minutes. So when we got to the next puddle, I lifted her up and proposed to carry her across. That was in the best traditions of Raleigh, wasn't it? But she kicked and screamed and unfortunately I stumbled and we both sat there, until a policeman came along and wished to know whether we were taking a *bain* in the middle of the *rue*?

Well, we made it up that night in bed – Yvonne always softened in bed – and I thought maybe that cold *Sitzbad* had cured her. But no, she still wanted me to act like a cross between Sir Galahad and the Duke of Buckingham as he figured in the novels of Dumas. She was always reading some new book about history and picked up new ideas as to how her perfect knight should behave. She wanted me to kiss her hand and it was all right as long as I could pass on to other, more interesting things. But if I didn't do it right, with the proper respect and delicacy, she held her fingertips under my nose and slapped me when I passed beyond her wrist. She declared that I ought to write poetry and had I read Ronsard and Bertrand de Born and what about entering a joust with her colours over my heart? I told her that an Englishman fought with his fists and how silly I would look with a great big lance in my hand; but she said she only meant it in a symbolic way and what was important was that I should fight for her honour like a knight of olden times.

We almost had a real fight but I happened to meet some old friends of mine from Bradford and Yvonne's brother came to Paris from Arles and we went out to celebrate. Now Yvonne was particularly intent on impressing her brother how happy we were and how wonderful a marriage she had made (for of course the family had disapproved of her picking a perfidious Englishman for her husband) so she acted the most loving wife and I thought everything was fine. But suddenly she frowned and looked at me and said:

'That man . . . in the corner . . . he is looking at me.'

I did not bother to turn round. '*Chérie*,' I said, 'all men like to look at a pretty woman. This, to coin a phrase, is a free country.'

But she lifted her little nose again and looked three kinds of daggers at me.

'*Pouf!*' she said, 'is that how you care for me? He is not only looking – he is winking!'

'That's serious,' I replied. 'But perhaps the poor fellow has a nervous tic. Let us not be too harsh on him.'

'*Salaud!*' cried Yvonne. 'If you do not go instantly and tell him to stop, I . . . I'll go myself!'

Pierre, Yvonne's brother, who speaks no English, was beginning to show great curiosity and demanded a translation. And I knew that the situation was serious, my wife suffering one of her attacks of romantic visions. Maybe that man wasn't winking. But if I didn't go over to him, I would soon find Yvonne winking at someone else.

So I went over and stopped in front of the table. The fellow was broadshouldered and had a red beard. His eyes were perfectly normal, only rather frosty. He looked up at me and I saw if he got up, he would be considerably taller than I – and I am almost six foot myself.

'Monsieur,' I addressed him politely, 'the lady in my company thinks you are ogling here. Please desist.'

'What?' he roared. 'Tell the lady to mind her own business.'

Now, this got me angry because he said it in a nasty tone.

Also, he used a word before 'business' which I did not like at all, in French, English or any other language.

'Restrain yourself, my friend,' I told him. 'Don't get excited.'

But he did not restrain himself. He felt obviously insulted. And in the end I slapped his face – what I could find of it under the flaming beard. And he flung a card at me though I did not know why we must get introduced at such a late stage.

'I'll expect your seconds without fail,' he said and stalked out of the bistro. But on his way he stopped at our table, swept off his big, broad-brimmed sombrero and said to Yvonne: 'My sympathies, madame. What a pity that you shall be such a young widow!'

I thought that Yvonne would be angrier than ever but she looked at me with shining eyes and whispered: 'My hero!' which sounded nice only I did not feel like it.

'A duel!' she went on, clapping her hands. 'It is wonderful.'

'And what if I am killed?' I asked. 'Have you thought of that?'

For a moment she looked distressed but then she said:

'I look very nice in black. But,' she added quickly in French, 'you won't be killed. You'll kill *him*!'

And then Pierre said in a choking voice: 'I am not so sure of that, 'and shoved the card across the table. I had dropped it and he had picked it up.

I looked at it and did not feel very cheerful. The card said:

THE GREAT CASCANI
William Tell's only genuine successor

Cirque Hippique, Paris

'I think we go back to Bradford,' I said. 'We can catch the train first thing tomorrow morning...'

'What do you mean?' squealed Yvonne. 'You cannot do that! This is a matter of honour.'

'I'm willing to trade honour for a whole skin,' I answered. 'Do you know who Cascani is? The best shot in the world.

He can put out three candles with one shot without cutting the wicks. He can shoot a dry pea from the tip of your nose at a hundred yards. He . . . '

'And you slapped him first,' said Pierre gloomily. 'Therefore he has the choice of weapons.'

Later when they got me up from the floor, I tried to reason to Yvonne. But how could you reason with a woman who expects a man to be a cross between King Arthur and Cyrano de Bergerac? And so I asked Pierre to find another friend and talk to Cascani. Perhaps . . . but I knew there was no 'perhaps'.

They agreed that we should all meet in the Bois de Boulogne the day after next, at dawn. Yvonne was terribly happy. She kissed me with considerable talent and abandon. But she would not listen to reason – even though I had bought the train and steamer tickets.

On the contrary, she insisted that we all went to the circus. I was considerably averse to sawdust and animals in any number but not even Pierre could help me; he said that it was better for me to know what I was up against.

So we went to the circus and there were various turns that left me colder than a comic doing the fiftieth imitation of Little Tich or George Robey except that now and then I jumped in my seat when Yvonne pinched me in her excitement. For she was highly excited and praised in equally extravagant terms the trained seals, the clowns and the equestrian performers.

Cascani was the big attraction. He appeared in a cape lined with red silk, smoking a cigar. He was even taller and more sinister under the spotlights and I began to think that perhaps, after all, I'd better take the next train even without Yvonne. But she sat next to me and when she didn't pinch me, she made to love to me and I decided that the least I could do was to die like a hero, an action for which I did not have any opportunity since I was almost sent to South Africa.

A very pretty girl in tights brought in a basket of apples. Beautiful red apples, polished to the utmost perfection. Cascani, it seemed, was crazy about apples. The very pretty girl put them on her head, one after the other. And he shot them off, one after the other. First standing, then kneeling, then bending down, then lying on his stomach – there was practically no posture of the human body, natural or unnatural, from which he could not hit an apple right in its core from any distance he chose.

I felt faint and I decided to slip out without watching the rest of Cascani's act. But when I picked up Yvonne and Pierre after the performance in the bar across the street, they told me that Cascani could remove the pips in the ten of diamonds, one by one, without spoiling the card unduly, that he . . . But at this point I asked them to stop; which they very kindly did.

Pierre came to fetch me in the morning and I never hated to get up so much, not even in school but he said I had to be on time. And Yvonne got up, too. When I said that women were not supposed to attend duels, she shrugged and asked whether I considered her just like any other woman? I couldn't answer that and we went downstairs. It seemed that there was plenty of time after all, and Yvonne was hungry.

'I am going to my death and you think of your stomach,' I complained but she just smiled and we went to a workers' café.

The breakfast was not continental but very elaborate and I sat there and watched Yvonne and Pierre gorge themselves with *café au lait* and *beurre* and *pain,* also bacon-and-eggs and fruit. Especially fruit. Yvonne had three oranges and she would have eaten grapes, too, only Pierre said, we must go. And I stared at the fruit bowl with a glazed look in my eyes and then did something I suppose sleepwalkers do or kleptomaniacs, only I paid for it because as usual I had to settle the bill.

And then were were in the Bois and Cascani was already waiting. He had two seconds and there was also a doctor. I walked across the grass with Pierre and Pierre's friend who was a man with a bad squint but otherwise a very honest deputy assistant registrar of the Twelfth Arrondissement – or so Pierre told me. I wanted to walk on – it was a beautiful morning – but Pierre told me to stop. He and the others got together, only I and Cascani stood and stared as if we had never seen anything as interesting as two fellows determined to fill each other with holes.

After a while we were led to each other and we were turned back to back as if we were going to play some party game. Then we were told to take twenty paces, turn and wait. First I was going to fire and then Cascani. This was a good thing because if Cascani had fired first I wouldn't have had a dog's chance to press the trigger.

So I fired. I heard a scream. It was Yvonne and a small bird's nest sat on her chic little hat which it seemed I had brought down with remarkable markmanship, without even taking aim. Then Cascani slowly lifted his pistol and I looked at him. I looked at him and sweated because I saw that he was taking aim at a strictly essential point of my anatomy. And then my fingers touched something in my pocket. It was a round and cold object and before I knew what I was doing I took the apple from my pocket and placed it on my head where it stayed, thank God.

I watched Cascani's face. It was twisted in a terrible grimace. I knew exactly what was happening inside him and my heart sang. Not quite loudly, but pianissimo. It was his personal dislike of me fighting with his professional pride and training. It was like one guardian angel fighting one fiend. And who won? Was this a Sunday school parable or real life, cold and damp, in the Bois? What do you think?

Cascani raised his pistol and I felt little pieces of apple trickling down my neck. Then Cascani threw away his pistol in disgust and stalked off. And Yvonne, with the bird's nest still on her hat, was extremely close to me. So close that I could see she had been crying

'Oh, *chéri*!' she said, 'don't ever do it again! Don't ever risk your precious life! I know that you are incurably romantic but think of your little wife! What would I do if anything happened to you?'

Women! I ask you, my friends, is there any possible way of understanding them?

Sing of Death in Greece

It was after the midday meal that Theodosia suddenly clutched her breast of which a score of poets had sung, which a dozen sculptors had modelled in Parian marble. She pressed her living flesh as if she wanted to keep life itself from fleeing. But her small hands with the long narrow fingers that had been kissed by young lips and old lips, by singer and tyrant, athlete and priest, were too weak. Before the evening shadows fell, Theodosia was dead.

Her wailing servants laid her on the flower-covered bier and hung purple-tongued torches above her. Their tears and their screams soon ceased for they were frightened of death, sudden and unreasonable, slipping like a treacherous assassin into the bed-chamber of the loveliest haetera in Athens, in all Greece, in all the civilised world. They crouched, shivering at the foot of the bier.

The news of her death soon spread. After the evening banquet some of her friends came to view the corpse; Leontes and Sophronisba, Brasidas the general and Laconia, his mistress. There was a large crowd and the cloying sweetness of the flowers mingled with their breath and their talk.

'Poor Theodosia,' said Laconia, trembling a little, realising for the first time in her twenty-three summers that she, too must die.

Brasidas bent over the bier.

'She is still beautiful,' he said. 'Strange – this is the first time that she sleeps alone. But she had her beauty and her lovers. She had a good life.'

But Laconia dug her sharp nails into his arm because he dared to speak lightly in the presence of death. Brasidas slapped her, gently, for he was fond of her. Then they all left and others came until the flood became a trickle and the trickle a drop or two. And then no one came.

But late at night when the torches were burning low the soul of Theodosia slipped from her cooling body. It was a tiny soul, hardly the size of a midge; forlorn and helpless it hovered over the bier, circled the dimly-lit chamber, searched for an opening and with a plaintive humming flew into the starlit warm night.

Yet it could not leave the house and the garden. Something drew it back into the room, back to the marble-like, lovely body. For the last time it wanted to see the flesh and curve that was Theodosia. She had been always in love with her body, her most precious possession and found it flattering that others shared this love. The soul-midge swept down, passed close to the lifeless form and rose again in sudden alarm.

A man was kneeling at the side of the bier. His broad shoulders shook in repressed sobs. It was Menander, Theodosia's first lover. The only one who loved her in death as in life, the only one who had not come to gape in vulgar curiosity. His grief was private and almost silent; but now and then he called her name, his voice broken and tear-choked.

Then, in a sudden paroxysm of grief, he took his dagger and plunged it into his heart.

The midge that was Theodosia's soul took fright at this violence. With a last, lingering look at the white body, it fled from the chamber. Outside there were millions of midges, myriads of souls streaming towards the stars. But their migration was not orderly; in confused swarms they hovered, retreated and swept on again. There was no clearly marked path, no signpost to guide them.

Theodosia's soul was bewildered and lonely. It tried to ask the way but the other souls were intent on their own progress and gave no answer. Her plaintive humming became fainter and fainter. It was lost.

Somewhere in that multitude was the soul of Menander. He, too, was freed of the burdens of the flesh. He, too, was seeking his way. But more than the path, he was searching for Theodosia.

They never met. In the thick, swirling cloud of soul-midges they passed and re-passed each other without recognition. For they had never looked at each other's souls while they lived; Theodosia did not believe in hers and Menander had tried in vain to find a way in which to show his own. Their souls were strangers and the midges merged into the deepening night, their humming, plaintive voices calling to each other in vain.

The Captain's Moustache

1

Fatima, of whom I can now tell the truth because I believe she no longer lives in Paris, was a rare and admirable beauty. I can quote several of my eminent colleagues, all experienced connoisseurs of feminine charms in corroboration of this statement. Her pure race, her nobility was clearly marked upon her delightful face, the delicate curve of her nose with the flaring nostrils whose colour was that of rose-petals; and those who spent a few coppers to watch this beauty were by no means idiots or boobies. For the sight of living beauty is benediction for the eyes and comfort for the soul.

Fatima's figure was both slim and voluptuous, a rare enough combination. She was an accomplished dancer and as her costume was not much larger than a handkerchief, it was a tribute to her perfect circulation that she never caught a cold. Her father's name was Ali-Men-Tootoo-Alla-Garen who never weighed less than three hundred and fifty pounds before he broke his fast. This meal consisted usually of half-a-sheep and the appropriately lavish garnishings, including half a hundredweight of potatoes. Fatima herself was surrounded by strange characters who scratched on hollow pumpkins and pounded on pigskins, calling the result music. Was she really a Tunisian? Only the learned students of Arabic could tell. Most people claimed that she was born within a stone's throw of the Cannabière, as Marseillaise as the song of the revolution. But she was dark-haired with eyes of midnight, with sudden languors, with truly Oriental nonchalance; she loved perfumes and unguents, was deliciously lazy, smiled at everybody with dazzling white teeth; having finished her dance, she moved with perfect grace through her audience, clinking the money she had already collected in the velvet bag she held out. Even in her most intimate encounters she never parted from a small silver box which contained a magic depilatory cream – a cream which she used to remove the faintest down from her arms and legs, from her upper lip and from the perfect miniature hillock under her navel. For the women of the tribe to which she claimed to belong were proud of being as smooth and as polished as the statues of ancient Greece.

My friend Jacques was madly in love with her and the noble daughter of Ali-Men-Tootoo-Alla-Garen condescended to share, almost every night, his bed once she had finished her performance. Let those who wish mock at such joys! The Venus of the Market Place can be just as delightful as the most aristocratic lady of the perfumed boudoirs.

2

I am sure you do not expect me to outrage the conventions of modesty and described in too graphic detail, course by course, game by game, blow by blow, one of those nights of Oriental passion. Jaques was a lucky fellow. His neighbour was a former soprano of the Sistine Chapel who, at an early stage of his career, had sacrificed his manhood for his art. Vulgar people called him a castrate; he described himself as a martyr of sacred music. His presence gave the coupling of Fatima and my friend that Moslem aroma, that Ottoman flavour which only powerful and obese pashas are supposed to enjoy and the hours melted away like the sweet pastilles of the seraglio, the quickly-devoured squares of Turkish delight. But let us not linger too long with the lovers. At a certain tragic point of time the lovely lady left the bed of her lover in order to perform her celebrated belly-dance in front of the gaping tourists. Or, if you want me to be classical, the abdominal Terpsychore descended from the Olympus to the Paradise of Mohamed. Their parting was so passionate and tumultuous that Fatima forgot on the mantelshelf the small silver box of which I have spoken and which contained the powerful unguent she used to remove the softest little hairs from her adorable body.

Fifteen minutes later there was a discreet knock on Jacques's door.

It is truly painful that I must make such a disclosure but an honest chronicler cannot hide the truth. This friend of mine whom I loved like a brother – and whom I was supposed to resemble to a striking extent – this extraordinary young man was an abominable lecher! He had *two* mistresses at the same time which is always imprudent – because they might, by some tragic coincidence, die at the same time and a wise man always has a third one in reserve to replace the dear departed. Well, I have got it out now, so don't feel too upset. She who knocked on the door and who entered a moment later was a pretty Parisienne called Angela de Minetcourtois. Was she truly of the nobility? I couldn't tell you. She used to relate how one of her ancestors whom the infidels had captured during one of the Crusades had risen to become Shah of Persia. But this important historical event remains undocumented – even though Angela also claimed that her ancestor had taken the name of Shah Poly. I believe that she had similar origins to that of Fatima. Women seem to be eager of making people believe that they were born in some other spot than their actual birth-place. For the peace of mind of men sometimes it would be better if they hadn't been born at all!

3

'I must take you to task, my love,' said Jacques, looking severely at the lovely Angela de Minetcourtois who was already sitting at the foot of his bed. The scent of Fatima was still lingering in a lukewarm cloud around them.

'You're still jealous, sir?'

'Certainly – and with good reason, my beautiful. I really have enough of your familiarity with Captain Manistrou. His moustache is getting on my nerves.'

'Manistrou! Captain Manistrou! You're jealous of that poor Manistrou? But you are a fool, my dear Jacques. He is a coxcomb, spending most of his time tugging at that twin piece of fleece which Nature happened to bestow upon his upper lip! That phoney gipsy who combs his hair like a savage Hungarian and can't turn his head without pricking somebody's nose with those hooks of hair which stick out from his cheeks like the points of a circumflex accent! How little you know me, Jacques Moulinot! I only love artists and poets; I abhor soldiers . . . '

'What a liar you are! As if I hadn't seen you, with my own eyes, in a mirror which you failed to notice, your lips glued to that creature you are supposed to abhor – that living hat-stand! Those moustaches could be used to hang your hat on – that's about all they're good for – and yet . . . '

'You're mistaken, Jacques, I'll swear – you must have taken some other woman for me. My darling, are we met here to argue about moustaches? Have we nothing better to do?'

'Certainly we have!' replied Jacques, mollified and, taking her in his arms, began to undress her with skill and dispatch. As he was in bed himself, he did not have to waste time undressing. He peeled off Angela's clothes and she emerged, rosy, shapely and impatient for love.

4

As she finished dressing after their prolonged and pleasurable encounter, Angela gave Jacques a final kiss. Then, raising her eyes, she noticed the small silver box which Fatima had forgotten on the mantelshelf.

'What's that?' she asked, with a slight frown.

To tell the truth, Jacques hadn't the faintest idea of the purpose of the unguent the box held. He thought it was one of the thousands of creams which pharmacists have invented against pimples and abrasions and which sometimes make their fortune – a far more important consideration to them than the succouring of the sufferings of humanity.

'That? It's a cream my doctor has given me against chapped lips or the inflammation of the gums . . . '

'Does it work?'

'Perfectly. It refreshes the skin, smoothes the wrinkles, it's a tonic, it's an astringent, it's a sweetener all at once. At

106

least that's what my doctor told me and I haven't yet caught him in a lie.'

'That's wonderful! You must give it to me . . . I suffer so much from the cold . . . my skin is so delicate . . .'

Jacques thought that the silver box wasn't quite a suitable present. But there are moments in which a man feels so grateful to a woman that she cannot ask for anything he would refuse – especially if she is already holding the thing in her small, capable hands.

Angela slipped the box into her pocket, pressed her forehead to the lips of Jacques and then disappeared like a fluttering bird, leaving a trace of the scent of verbena behind her.

Two days later Jacques met a friend. It was Yvan de Noffés, a delightful native of Périgord.

'When did you last see Captain Mainistrou?' he asked Jacques.

'Why?' Jacques replied with a question, showing singularly little enthusiasm.

'Because if you met him now, you wouldn't recognise him.'

'He no longer looks like the idiot he is?'

Oh yes – but he has lost his moustache, his celebrated moustache!'

'He . . . he cut it off?'

'Oh no . . . it dropped off by itself. He went to sleep with it and next morning . . .'

In the meantime Fatima had revealed to Jacques the proper purpose of the unguent which she thought she had lost. And now a wide grin split my friend's face.

'At least Angela can't tell me that she's never been kissed by the captain on the lips . . .'

And then another idea occurred to him.

'But maybe she used the cream the same way as Fatima did? And maybe the captain . . .'

It didn't really matter, he reassured himself. One way or other the hirsute captain had lost his manly pride, his male ornament. And if that cream was truly efficacious, the moustache would never sprout again!

The Japanese Vase

People are funny.

I was walking down Piccadilly when someone called my name. I turned to see a tall, grey-haired, brown-skinned man with a friendly smile upon his face. His teeth were very white; the whole man had a charm which even members of his own sex experienced – and women thought irresistible.

'You don't recognise me, do you?' he asked.

'I'm afraid I don't.'

'I am Dick Boughey. We met about five or six years ago – up in Cark. We drank ale together.'

'Oh yes, of course. How are you, Dick?'

'I landed yesterday,' he continued. 'I don't suppose you know that I've been out East – China, Indonesia, Japan . . . '

'Yes, yes, I heard about it.'

'I'm settling down now in London and I hope we'll meet often. I hear we are both members of the same club.'

'That's fine, Dick. We must have lunch together, soon.'

'Do you know why I stopped you? I'd like to know your home address. Don't laugh at me – I brought you a little token, a present from foreign parts.'

'For me? That's really nice of you.'

'From Japan. Don't worry, it isn't anything particularly valuable. Just a vase.'

'You really make me feel embarrassed. I can't understand why . . . '

'I went down with malaria – four long months I was on my back. I'd have died of boredom but *you* saved me . . . '

'I?'

'Yes. Before I left, my sister put some of your books in my luggage – you know how she admires them. I hadn't read anything of yours before but during my convalescence I went through them all – well, most of them. They cheered me up no end, I can tell you . . .'

'Well, a sick man has little resistance,' I protested modestly.

'During all those days, camping out, I thought a lot of you. Gratefully. I decided then to give you the vase which I had bought in Japan and took with me to Celebes.'

I pressed Dick Boughey's hand. I was really moved.

'You're most kind,' I said. 'I'll be proud to have that vase. At least it will remind me that all my scribbling hasn't been in vain.'

I need hardly say that from that moment onwards I felt the deepest and warmest sympathy for the returned traveller.

'We'll soon meet again!'

We parted; and I forgot all about the Japanese vase. Evidently Boughey forgot about it, too. For six months I never heard of him. Then we ran into each other at Victoria. Boughey frowned when he saw me; then suddenly he brightened.

'Oh yes, I promised you something, didn't I?' he said. 'A Japanese vase? You'll get it, old chap, you'll get it. But you can't imagine how much trouble and worry I've had recently.'

'Really? What was the matter?' I asked.

'I had sixteen cases of stuff sent over. I had to unpack it and find the right place for every piece. But now, thanks to Buddha, I've finished the job. And I managed to find your vase, too. If you don't mind, I'll send it to you . . .'

'It isn't urgent. Any time that suits you . . .'

Boughey himself couldn't have considered the matter urgent; for weeks I heard nothing from him. And the vase didn't arrive. Then we happened to sit next to each other in Covent Garden. He blushed a little when he saw me but suddenly he shook my hand and said with bitter reproach: 'I must say . . . these English working-men . . . a fine lot?'

'Why, what's the argument about?' I asked.

'You know, that vase I brought for you from Japan . . . it is in a special sandalwood box. The lock was broken and

I gave it to the best locksmith . . . The trouble I had! My man has been to see him ten times but it still isn't fixed. At last I went there myself and he confessed that he had to send it up to Sheffield. I got it back today, at last; you'll have it tomorrow.'

I didn't have it. Another month passed. Yet I must confess that after hearing of the sandalwood box, I really became curious. I wanted that vase.

A month later we met in Regent Street. As soon as he saw me, he turned away his head and scurried into the next doorway where, I am sure, he had no business at all. I was getting really annoyed. Why should I have a Japanese vase? I didn't want the damn' thing. I've lived without one in the past; I could endure the future without it. This nice Boughey might come to hate me because of it.

A little later I ran into him by accident. It was on the Embankment of the Thames. When he saw me, his face distorted itself in painful embarrassment.

'I say,' he began, 'where on earth is that Tafford Street where you're supposed to live?'

'It's Stafford Street,' I replied, confused.

'So that's it!' the returned traveller cried. 'And I've been looking for Tafford Street for months!'

He took his diary from his pocket and put down Stafford Street, underlining the S three times. His face was red, he was gnawing at his moustache. He must have known that I saw through his little game and this humiliated and angered him. He didn't mention the vase this time – nor did he send it.

Last winter I met him at the Arlingtons. When I entered, his healthy colour turned a mottled white. He gave me a look full of despair and hate as if he meant to say: 'Can't I even have a drink without this miserable wretch spoiling it?'

He stepped up to me, grim and formal. 'By the way,' he said, 'did you get a Japanese vase from me?'

His daring startled me. 'Yes, I did,' I replied with shameless calm.

This surprised him. He bit his lip.

'I asked you,' he grunted, 'because I've discovered not

long ago that my man whom I've trusted for years, has been robbing me right and left.'

'The scoundrel!' I said to back him up.

'He stole quite a few Oriental curios which I gave him to take to some of my friends . . . So I didn't know whether he took that vase to you! . . . I strongly suspect that he didn't . . .'

Oh no, I thought, we won't start *that* game again. I'll finish with this blasted vase once and for all.

'I got the vase and I thanked you for it . . . I wrote a long letter,' I lied without batting an eye. 'But perhaps my letter was lost or your man kept it. It was a lovely Ming and . . .'

At this moment our hostess stepped up to us.

'Oh yes, the Ming vase!' she said. 'I saw it! Isn't it a beauty? Boughey showed it to us when we visited him yesterday with my husband . . . It was Ming, wasn't it?'

'That's a different vase,' murmured Dick Boughey. 'It isn't Ming . . .'

The lady smiled at him and said gaily:

'I am sure that vase reminds you of some unpleasant adventure. When I picked it up, you looked quite glum and later you covered it with a shawl . . . I'd give a lot to know the real story . . .'

Poor Boughey! How that vase must have tortured him!

I thought that with my merciful lie I had settled the matter forever but I soon found out my mistake. The vase wouldn't be buried. From that day onwards Boughey behaved as if I were his mortal enemy. He barely returned my greeting when we met. If we happened to run into each other at a party he showed an icy reserve.

The Arlingtons gave a dinner the other day. I was invited and accepted gladly for I like Sarah Arlington. Two days before the dinner she sent me a letter cancelling it. Later I found out to my surprise that the dinner had taken place – without me. But Boughey was there. What did it mean? Later several of my friends asked me confidentially in what way I had insulted or hurt Boughey. Whenever my name was mentioned in his presence, he turned gloomy, even angry. He never accused me of anything but neither did he make a secret of his opinion that he'd rather not sit at the same table with me.

Yesterday I met him in the street. I'll never forget the haughty, black and contemptuous look he gave me before he turned away his head. And last night as I crossed Oxford Street, a hansom cab almost ran me over. It missed me by a couple of inches. My first thought was: how relieved poor Boughey would be if he read in the papers tomorrow that I was dead and buried!

People are funny.

The Lesson

Crossing the hall with his rapid, loping stride, he saw the girl. He passed through the towering doors, walked slowly to the next corner and then turned back.

She was still sitting in the high-backed armchair. She rested her head on her small, gloved hand. She wore a thin golden bracelet and there was a shiny crocodile skin bag in her lap. She was enveloped in a light, evasive perfume; just a hint, hardly more than the scent of a single flower. She sat calmly, impassively.

For a while he paced the lush carpet restlessly; then he sat down, facing her. Impatiently he turned over the pages of a morocco-bound book. He drank in her perfume, and suddenly it became almost unbearable so that he could hardly breathe. He closed his book and looked at her as if he saw her for the first time.

She smiled.

The young man got up. There was suppressed excitement in his voice as he addressed her:

'Do you believe in mysterious, irresistible sympathies? Do you believe that human beings can be drawn to each other helplessly?'

The girl did not answer at once. There was a little sadness in her face, thoughtful and balancing.

'You mean this actually happened to you?' she asked with mingled interest and irony.

He sat down in the chair beside her. He lit a cigarette and killed the match with a nervous gesture.

'Every man carries the image of a woman whom he has created and whom he cannot find. And now I come down from my room, look up from my book, quite absent-mindedly – and here you are!'

The girl lowered her eyes and smiled. She seemed to be toying with some obscure, inexpressible idea.

'And this is a good enough excuse to accost me – just like that?' She shrugged. 'Why, anyone could do that – whether he believes in your theory or not.'

'If I only saw a pretty girl in you,' he argued, 'you would be perfectly right. But I suddenly sensed something . . . don't laugh at me, please. Your mind, your soul, your whole feminine being . . . That's why I had to do it. If I had been shy, if I hadn't spoken to you, maybe we wouldn't ever have met . . .

'And if I were ugly?'

'But you aren't. You are . . . '

'Still, suppose I became suddenly plain?'

'It couldn't make any difference – now. Not any more.'

Again she fell silent, retiring into her thoughts.

'Are you waiting for someone?' the young man asked.

'Yes.'

'Your husband?'

She smiled.

'Or your lover?'

'You're going much too fast.'

'Listen . . . What is your name?'

'Ann.'

'Ann. I love you.'

She took a deep breath. 'But you don't even know me.'

He took her hand and pressed it.

'Still: I love you.'

The girl had no time to answer. A pageboy had walked up to her. There was a message for her at the desk. Yet the young man was certain she would come back. And then they could go on –

There was a brightness in the girl's eyes, a smile on her lips. Then she leaned to the right, grasped the arm of the chair and slowly, painfully she raised herself. And as she started, she dragged her left foot after her as if it were an alien body, a strange burden.

'She's lame!' cried the young man to himself.

At once he decided to get up and leave. It was true feminine depravity to sit here, maybe for hours, hiding her lameness behind a motionless, attractive pose; wait for some stupid victim who might continue the unwilling comedy of love because of male chivalry or false pity. He was about to get up when he saw the girl approaching him – limping towards him, a bright smile on her lips.

She wanted to speak but as she looked at him, she stopped, startled – as if she understood everything. For a few seconds they sat silently, side-by-side. She stared into the air. He clenched his hands and hit the arms of the chair in an irritated gesture.

'Listen,' he began in a condescending tone, 'however painful a subject, I must . . . .'

Her face quivered.

'Please, don't go on.'

'But you understand, don't you? After all, I . . .

The girl nodded quickly.

'It's my fault. But you started so nicely. I believed that it was . . . still . . . possible. That even I can . . . ' She bent her head and whispered softly: ' . . . that even a miserable cripple . . . '

The young man was reassured by this quick resignation. He presented her with a few words of consolation; a somewhat drooping bouquet of words. He said that he had the greatest sympathy for her. She was a charming girl. He would be delighted if they met again some time – to talk like two good friends. There was nothing finer in the world than genuine, disinterested friendship. Any time at all – any other time. But now he was terribly sorry, he had to rush; he was already late for an important business appointment.

She looked at him pleadingly.

'There are . . . others . . . around us. If you went away, they would all think . . . they would all know . . . that you left me. If you would wait a few minutes . . . someone's coming to fetch me, you see?'

He nodded with sulky resignation. They exchanged a few empty phrases; the conversation was dragging. Sometimes the girl looked at him with a silent, warm smile; but the young man's face was cold and empty and he could hardly wait to get away.

A tall, well-dressed man stopped at the bottom of the sweeping staircase. He looked around, searchingly. The girl's face brightened. She raised her gloved hand.

'Alex! Here I am! Alex!'

Then she jumped up suddenly and smiled at the young man, a trifle ironically.

'I was very happy to talk to you,' and she offered her hand. 'It was nice of you to keep me company until my husband came.'

Then she took the other man's arm and walked away. She was no longer limping or dragging her foot. She was straight like a slim tree, walking with soft, feminine certainty and grace.

The young man got up and started out hesitantly after them. He would have liked to shout; but they had already disappeared through the portal-like doors. He stood there for a long time, his eyes staring, his fingers quivering. He felt as if the dream of beauty had slipped through his hand, faded into nothing. He recalled every word and every gesture and his face flushed red with humiliation.

He thought that it had been a good lesson. But he also thought that all women were fiends in human shape and that he would *never* find one who possessed a soul . . .

Adventure in Scheveningen

1

For many years M. René Dupont, *avocat* of the sixteenth
arrondissement in Paris, hadn't taken a holiday. For almost
a decade he hadn't left his dusty office but instead, sweated
and toiled through August. His secretary and mistress,
Huguette Leblanc, pleaded in vain for a little trip, a small
vacation; yet the answer was always the same:

'We can't afford it this year. Maybe next.'

'We never go away, I know we never shall,' replied
Huguette plaintively. 'We'll die here in the heat.'

Maitre Dupont usually didn't listen to the last words,
masking his face with letters and documents.

'Go alone, Huguette,' he said. 'I don't care if you go to
Le Touquet or the Midi or Switzerland. Choose a place yourself, I'll give you money, only don't pester me. I can't go
this year . . . '

'So you'd let me go alone . . . '

Dupont glanced up.

'Of course I would. When are you leaving?'

'Aren't you worried . . . ?'

'Nobody will steal you!' laughed the *avocat*.

'I understand,' replied Huguette grimly. 'I understand
only too well. You want to get rid of me so that you can
enjoy yourself with those horrible creatures . . . '

'What *are* you talking about?'

'About your bare-armed girl friends who keep on sending you messages to meet their friends from the *demi-monde*
in the Bois.'

Dupont shrugged.

'You're mad,' he said. 'You're crazy.'

'For twelve years I've suffered here in this office. You never take me anywhere, winter or summer: I'm breathing the dust in this dark hole – every year you promise we'll go. I can't imagine how I stood these twelve years . . . '

Maitre Dupont was used to these dramatic sceenes. He and Huguette had been together such a long time, not a day passed without tears and reproaches. And it was getting worse. Two years ago Huguette only shed tears; last year she got the hiccoughs and fainted. This year she had a 'heart-attack' and had to go to bed. (Maitre Dupont put cold compresses on her chest.) And all this because of the summer holidays.

He and Huguette had been lovers for eleven years. Huguette said twelve but this small mathematical error was pardonable. (Like the slip of the waiter's pencil adding up the bill.)

2

Dupont kept on promising a summer holiday until this year he decided to pay the long-standing debt. They went to Scheveningen. It was crowded and they had to stay at the distinguished Hotel Wilhelmus; the only rooms left were the bridal suite which consisted of two bedrooms, a sitting room, a study and two bathrooms. Truly a princely suite which even boasted of a valet's bedroom.

Maitre Dupont was not a man of impressive exterior. Though he was rich and making a lot of money, he didn't care for appearances; he was much too clever and intelligent to ascribe any importance to well-pressed trousers and well-built suits. His clothes were always crumpled, his hat battered and shabby as if it had just been run over by a car.

The velvet collar of his overcoat had been almost worn bare; but at Scheveningen nobody objected to it. They had seen plenty of shabby millionaires. M. Dupont was considered a wealthy eccentric; his frayed trousers did not make his custom less valuable. The Dutch have always been realists; they prefer the tips to be princely however *petit bourgeois* appearances may be.

3

Nor was Huguette one of the ten best dressed women of Europe. She was a modest girl who had her clothes made in small *salons*. She sometimes actually wore the same hat for two years running.

Such things were unusual in Scheveningen. Here they were used to the ladies of the most crumpled millionaires being dressed in silks and furs; and of course, their jewelry had to be stunning. Huguette had nothing at all except the small gold medallion hanging from a thin gold chain. Inside the medallion she had preserved Maitre Dupont's bespectacled snapshot photo with a circular stamp marking his nose for it had been originally used for his season ticket. In Scheveningen and especially in the Hotel Wilhelmus all females were covered with diamonds. Without jewelry these women felt positively naked.

So Huguette and her lover decided to buy some good paste jewelry. Huguette looked a little sour, she hated such stuff. But she realised that for a princely suite one needed jewels befitting a maharanee.

4

Dupont bought her a wonderful paste diamond bracelet, a huge 'diamond' ring and a phoney emerald necklace. The three pieces cost only a couple of hundred gulden.

That night the staff discussed Huguette's jewels in detail.

'They're worth at least half a million,' said one of the maids with expert knowledge.

'You're an idiot! They're worth a million and a half or more,' replied the floor waiter. 'The ring alone's worth half a million ...'

Poor, modest Huguette in her simple dresses which looked like a shabby coat with diamond buttons . . . She twinkled and dazzled, the whole of Scheveningen envied her for them.

'That's something!' they said. 'That's real wealth!'

119

In public Huguette wore her treasures with great dignity and seriousness. But inside the lovely apartment she dropped them on the floor, scattered them on the table; sometimes the maid picked them up from behind the bed, looking startled and horrified.

'That's just like these crazy millionaires,' she would say, 'Not taking the slightest care. I swear to you, I'm more worried about her jewelry. If something's lost, it's me who'll get into trouble, God forbid.'

And one day the dazzling diamond ring *did* get lost. The whole hotel feverishly started to search for it. Pageboys, maids, dived under the beds, the natives dug in the sand of the beach. The whole of Scheveningen was trying to restore to Huguette her wonderful treasure.

At noon the chief of police appeared at the hotel, questioned all the people concerned and told René Dupont that he would leave no stone unturned, that he staked his entire reputation on success. The diamond ring, worth a fortune, had to be found. Nothing ever had been lost in Scheveningen, he declared proudly if somewhat sweepingly.

In the meantime Huguette retired to her suite, afraid that she would burst out laughing into the police chief's face; the worthy official enquired excitedly where madame was as he wished to express his regrets.

'She has a headache,' replied Maitre Dupont. 'I'm sorry but she can't see anybody.'

'How she must be suffering!' replied the chief of police. 'I understand. What a pity!'

Then he walked up to Huguette's closed door and called out to her:

'Even if it's at the bottom of the sea, I'll find it! Even if it's fathoms deep under sand, we'll dig it up! The police of Scheveningen takes its job seriously!'

6

For days they lived in terror – trembling that the ring would be found and the finder would discover that it's a fake.

'We've become tricksters quite innocently,' raged Maitre Dupont.

'If this becomes known, I'll die of shame!' added Huguette.

Maitre Dupont studied the Dutch criminal code. Luckily he found that the wearing of paste jewelry and passing them on as genuine was only punishable if someone acquired financial advantages by it with a view of causing damage or loss to others.

'Listen, let's not go on with this comedy,' said Huguette. 'I'll pack and we'll leave ... escape all this ... '

'You're to blame for everything,' said the *avocat*. 'You and your holidays abroad! Such a thing would have never happened to us at Le Touquet or ... '

'Of course I'm always to blame!' replied Huguette bitterly. 'On the other hand, you're a megalomaniac! Did we have to live in such a princely suite? Tell me – when you were a boy, did they beat you if you didn't pick the most expensive toy in the shop?'

7

While they went on quarrelling, they packed their suitcases quickly and could hardly await the moment when the train would take them away from Scheveningen.

It was their last day. Wherever they walked, the sympathetic and consolatory looks of people accompanied them; people stepped off the pavement, opened their ranks to them so that they could pass in peace and in their great grief.

The whole of Scheveningen was bending over ashcans, digging under bushes, in the sand, seeking the ring.

The police spent the night in the quest; for days the fishermen had kept close to the shore; they were casting not for fish but for the ring.

The pages of the hotel sprawled on their stomachs along the gutters, crawled under chairs.

'*Mon Dieu*, if only they won't find it for another twelve hours,' muttered Maitre Dupont, his lips pale. 'By that time we'll be across the frontier.'

They said goodbye. Dupont shook hands with the head porter who apologised, stuttering and embarrassed, for the great loss that had befallen the honoured guests.

'I still hope it'll be found. The whole police and all the firemen are doing nothing but looking for it.'

Maitre René Dupont scarcely heard him. He asked for the luggage and shouted furiously at Huguette who was rummaging under the beds, opening drawers, finding new and new small articles; a handkerchief or two in the bed, a comb behind the tub, slippers in the bed-side cabinet . . .

These are the usual small tricks which the staff employs even in the most distinguished hotels. God forbid that they should steal anything – but they hide handkerchiefs, studs, half-empty bottles of perfume, a pair of silk stockings in drawers which nobody uses. If these things are found, nobody can reproach them; but usually the departing guests fail to notice them, leave them behind and the maids or bellboys 'inherit' them.

Huguette was going through these 'neglected' drawers while René Dupont stood at the desk and phoned up several times to speed her up.

'Come on, the devil take that rubbish, we'll miss the train – and I don't want to stay here another day . . .'

The hall porter asked for M. Dupont's Paris address and put it down in a big book, remarking sadly:

'I still hope we can find that ring . . .'

They rushed to the station and walked up and down the platform.

'I wish that train were in!' Maitre Dupont's face was red with excitement. 'It's no use,' he added, 'we aren't good tricksters. No talent for crime at all.'

At last the train arrived at the platform and the excited couple took their places happily in a reserved compartment.

The conductor collected their sleeping car tickets and their passports.

Huguette stepped into the corridor, waiting for the moment of departure with well-simulated calmness.

'Six minutes!' said the conductor.

'That we can somehow survive,' said Maitre Dupont and buried his nose in a newspaper.

The next moment Hugette screamed softly.

'Stop! Wait! Monsieur René Dupont! Where's M. Dupont?'

All passengers crowded to the window. It was a police inspector, followed by several policemen and a fireman or two, not to mention a detachment of the hotel staff.

'M. Dupont, M. Dupont, we've found the ring!'

Tremendous sensation; the engine driver climbed from his cab; conductors, travellers, all surrounded Maitre Dupont.

'The ring's been recovered! A frogman found it, near the hotel. It's now at police headquarters, locked in the safe . . . You must come back, M. Dupont. There's a statement to be signed – and the Chief of Police insists on handing over the ring himself.'

10

They removed the luggage. M. René Dupont left the train with the dejected face of a burglar who was caught at the last moment with the swag.

It was a triumphal procession to police headquarters. They took solemn possession of the phoney ring which shone with a brilliance as if to mock at its happy owners. They had to look happy, too; then it was a matter of reaching deep into Maitre Dupont's pockets – the rewards! M. Dupont who was uninformed about the suitable payment to an honest finder, asked the Chief of Police.

'I think ten thousand won't be too much – but that diver deserves more! You're still getting off well. That ring's worth half a million to anybody.'

The *avocat* forked out the ten thousand. A painful silence. The hotel staff also expected a little tip.

'Yes, yes, of course, I'll pay everything . . . Only let's get to the station – or we'll miss the train.'

'The station? The next train leaves at eleven fifty-five tonight.'

The manager of the hotel bent close to Dupont's ear.

'Monsieur – a good lunch for the boys and girls! They've been searching for three days!'

The champagne flowed. Huguette sat at the head of the table with the frogman-diver's wife beside her. At the other end Maitre Dupont was still distributing money. At this moment the chief representative of the local insurance company arrived, beginning forthwith to pitch his sales talk, trying to persuade Dupont to insure the jewels – for a minimum of two million gulden.

The radio was blaring out the Nutcracker Suite. The noise was so bad that no one could hear himself speaking. Everybody was happy, everybody was rewarded. Only Huguette was crying. The diver's wife bent close to her and whispered confidentially:

'I understand, madame . . . the tears of joy!'

The Model Husband

By a general consensus of opinion, of all my friends Ernest is the best, most attentive husband. He is still as kind and gentle to his wife as if they were on their honeymoon. And yet they had been married for almost fourteen years.

Truly a model husband. Sometimes he'll jump from an omnibus or stop his hansom cab just to buy his wife flowers from a street-barrow. He seldom sees her in the morning for she likes to sleep late while Ernest has to be at his office by nine sharp. But he always goes home for lunch. He never forgets to remark how lovely she looks, how beautifully her new dress suits her. He requests detailed information about her night's sleep, her general state of health and probes gently whether, God forbid, she had had some annoyance or upset during the morning. Ernest not only remembers birthdays, wedding anniversaries and all the other important milestones – a fortnight before each date he starts a searching investigation among Madge's girl-friends to discover her secret desires and ascertain the nature of the gift that would give her the greatest pleasure. Whenever Madge loses her temper – which happens now and then as she has a rather short one – and makes a slightly insulting remark in company, hurting someone's susceptibilities, Ernest immediately swings into action. He backs Madge up to the hilt but finds opportunity to console the injured party, talks to him, cajoles him until ruffled vanity is smoothed and peace restored. Whatever Madge does, must be right – not only right but excellent and admirable – in Ernest's eyes.

Yesterday we met at a dinner party. As we knew that we were all invited, we agreed to go there together. Ernest has no carriage but he wouldn't dream of letting Madge travel by hansom on such occasions. Something might happen to her evening dress, some boor might step on her delicate evening slippers. As my flat was on their way, Ernest told me that they would pick me up in their brougham.

He came up to my flat and while we walked downstairs, he said in a voice bursting with enthusiasm:

'Madge has a great surprise for us!'

'Surprise?'

'She has a new evening dress . . . I haven't seen it myself. She only brought it home late this afternoon. She wouldn't let me look at her but slipped on her fur coat. You can imagine how curious I am!'

I couldn't feel as thrilled and excited as he did – but then, I didn't have to pay Madge's bills. (For which small mercies etc.) I said something civil. When I got into the carriage, Madge sat there wrapped up in her fur coat and of the dress there was nothing to be seen.

But in the hall of the house to which we were invited, she took off her furs. I must confess that I was staggered. I had never seen such a daringly low-cut dress in all my life. I don't want to sound like a prig and I know that every woman loves to enjoy her own beauty – and its effect on men. But this dress was no joking matter. In front – well, it just touched the borderline of scandal. In the back – it wasn't a décolletage. It just didn't exist, that's all. We knew that Madge had a lovely back. Now we discovered that she had beautiful hips, too. Nor was it any longer a secret that about an inch below her waist line, exactly over her spine, there was a tiny brown mole.

Madge stood there triumphantly, a happy smile on her small face. She turned round so that we could see her in all her glory – and a bit more. I looked at Ernest. Ernest swallowed hard. Very hard. He almost swallowed his Adam's apple.

'Lovely dress,' he said politely. But there was no real enthusiasm in his voice.

We joined the party. Madge's dress was a real sensation. It startled everybody. The ladies made honeyed remarks with the appropriate sting hidden in them. One of them said:

'How fortunate you are, my pet. My husband would box my ears if I put on a dress like this – though there's nothing to it.'

Behind her the men grinned. Some of the younger guests, when Ernest wasn't looking, inspected Madge's back and hips, not to speak of the mole, with such impudent interest that it was really a scandal and might have led to an ugly row. All evening Madge's dress was the main topic of conversation. Unavoidably it led to a general argument. Ernest listened patiently for a while but when he had heard enough he declared in a voice of quiet authority:

'Dress is a private matter. If any ladies dislike my wife's clothes, they are simply envious. If any gentleman dislikes them, I'd like to hear his opinion.'

This ended the argument. If it concerned Madge, Ernest could be tough – and unpleasant. Those who had made catty remarks, were subdued. Someone brought up a different topic, the conversation was safely guided away from the décolletage. But the argument itself had spoiled the mood of the evening. Soon after eleven the party broke up. I left with Ernest and Madge. I was curious what the model husband would have to say once we were alone.

He was still the courteous, kind gentleman. He helped her into the cab, spread a rug over her knees, asked her whether she was comfortable, did all he ought to have done. Then he said:

'Darling, Charles and I are going to look in at the club for half-an-hour. But you'd better go straight home, *put on something and go to bed* ...'

Never before had I admired Ernest so much. And never before had I felt how difficult it was to remain a – model husband.

Orphan John

If there is poetic justice in the world, it stands to reason that there must be poetic injustice, too. To prove it, let me tell you the story of Orphan John whom I used to know in Budapest.

John was born in a hovel; his mother, being both poor and flighty, put him under a doorway and departed. She was a careful parent, though; she had wrapped him up in a warm shawl and pinned a note to it with the single word 'JOHN'. In the city orphanage he was given another name but we only knew him as Orphan John. As I said, he was given another name, but little else. He grew up like the sparrows and was just as poor.

Most of his life he spent in the streets. Or he sat in a cafe and looked out upon the street scene. Or he walked along the streets and stared into the cafes. Sometimes, especially during the slack periods, he sat behind one of the big plate glass windows and filled pages and pages with a fine, crabbed hand-writing. He wrote and wrote, mysteriously and indefatigably.

But sometimes when he got tired he took a book from his pocket and spent hours poring over it, tasting each page, flavouring each paragraph. This book was his only achievement; it bore, if not his name, at least his initials. Its cover had faded but the red letters were still faintly legible. 'HOW TO WRITE LOVE LETTERS by O.J.' they said.

At such times there was a faint smile on his haggard face. His eyes were shining grey like the Danube in the rain. Perhaps he was basking in the anonymous glory of the thought that thousands and thousands had declared their passions by using his words; the pink and blue stationery upon which his specimen letters had been copied flamed up like a bonfire in his heart.

One autumn day Orphan John rose from the cafe table a little unsteadily and hurried into the street. For years and years he had roamed the city, following the women who passed by, full of hope and heroic resolutions. At such times every word, every line of his compendium of letters surged and sang in his soul; he only needed a girl who would listen to him.

Sometimes he picked out one and followed her for hours – always from a safe distance. They gave him discouraging glances for Orphan John was not exactly handsome. Poverty was evident in his dress and behaviour; it made even his face less human. And gradually he got used to the fact that the more persistent he was the louder they laughed at him.

But John consoled himself always in the same way.

'Why should I court one woman so hard when there are thousands and thousands in my city? They all belong to me!'

And he no longer persisted in following a single girl; after a while he deserted the one he chose to track down another. Not that it was any use. It seemed that all women had entered a conspiracy not to have anything to do with him.

Yet no one was such an ardent admirer of femininity as he. A slim waist, a provocative curl, made his face burn as if in agony. The curve of a cheek, the shape of a neatly-shod foot made him feverish.

On this strange autumn evening he roamed the streets and felt all aglow with the thirst for love, the inner fire. Everywhere he seemed to encounter happy couples and lovers in each other's arms. He glanced into the suburban shops and saw lovely ladies behind the counters. Sometimes with a sudden effort, he went in, bought some small article and then left.

'How much for this cake of soap?' he asked in a tense, almost gasping voice. His eyes shone as if he had not eaten for a week.

'Tenpence,' replied the pretty shop girl and John paid for it without being able to find anything more to say. All his attempts at conversation were failures.

He was exhausted and found it hard to lift his feet. The city began to turn in for the night. Another few minutes and only such women would be abroad unaccompanied as he would not care to follow.

Orphan John felt that he had to hurry and make one last desperate attempt. In the last moment he noticed a girl hurrying along – a shop girl or a semptress she must have been, anxious to get home before the doors of the tenement house were locked up for the night and she had to tip the janitor to let her in. She was thin and no longer young; poverty and toil had robbed her of whatever beauty she might have possessed. But Orphan John followed her with the same enthusiasm as if she had been a fairy queen.

The girl did not look back and suddenly turned into a doorway. And like a drowning man clutching a straw, Orphan John quickly reached out to take her into his arms – and then, with a tender confession, remedy his rudeness.

Then at last she turned back and with loathing in her voice, hate on her face, cried:

'You miserable wretch! What do you take me for? Get away from me!'

The janitor was approaching already with his swaying lantern and the big bunch of keys. John hurried from the doorway; and the door was locked. The last door.

Hopeless and frustrated, he dragged himself along the broad boulevard and collapsed on a bench. Behind him there stood a large carriage whose interior was lit up. It had just stopped in front of a handsome villa which looked most romantic, as if it had been transferred to this place from some fairy tale world. It had small leaded windows through which lamplight came diffused in many colours.

As the porter opened the turquoise blue gate of the villa, a garland of electric bulbs was lit up above the door. In its bright glow a young woman appeared. Her white dress shone like the newly-fallen snow, the golden strands of her hair were dazzling and so were her emerald-green eyes. She walked softly, gliding along like a cat on padded feet. As she stepped up into the cab, Orphan John saw for a moment her slim ankles and a flash of pearly skin.

The next moment the door of the cab was closed and it started to move away.

Orphan John looked around carefully – then, like a thief, he tiptoed to the turquoise-blue gate. He caressed the wrought iron and pressed his burning lips against its coolness.

Suddenly, as he glanced down on the pavement, he saw something bright and glittering. He carried it under the nearest street lamp and saw that it was a tiny fan, hardly bigger than a tropical butterfly – but it shone in opalescent colours and was studded with diamonds. It was evident that the lady who had just left must have dropped it.

It wasn't honesty that urged Orphan John to turn it in – it was the thirst for love. This fan was a magic wand that would open the gates of the enchanted castle; perhaps he could arouse fairies from their sweetest dreams and find in some soft room the great adventure, the passionate love he had sought for years in vain.

He rang the bell. The turquoise-blue gate opened, the garland of electric bulbs came to brilliant life. A young woman appeared under them whose apron and starched hair-ribbon shone like the freshly-fallen snow and whose brown hair seemed to hide shadows of the bluest midnight. Her eyes were bright and her lips very red.

'What is it?' asked the pretty ladies' maid.

'I found something,' said Orphan John and his tongue almost clung to the roof of his mouth. 'I found this fan outside and brought it back . . . '

'Oh, it's madam's fan,' said the maid. 'They'd have blamed me for it, I am sure!'

She looked cross – but this made her face the prettier; it dimpled and became enchanting. Orphan John lost his mind in every one of her dimples.

'A pity she isn't at home,' the girl continued. 'You would have been paid a reward straight away. Come back tomorrow, I'll tell her what happened . . . '

'I want no reward,' he said proudly. 'I am rewarded beyond my dreams – just because I can see you, my fairy queen!'

The girl laughed.

'How silly you are! I am not a fairy queen nor anything as grand as you think. I am just a maid here; my name's Ilona Kincses.'

Now 'Kincses' means 'precious' in Hungarian and Orphan John thought that was a most fitting name for such a lovely girl. He repeated it with awe. Then he bent down and kissed her hand.

'Whatever you are,' he whispered, 'you are far more beautiful than your mistress . . .'

He really meant it. For the first time in his life he had met a girl who did not laugh at him, who listened to his burning words, his passionate phrases.

'I can see you are an honest man,' said Ilona. 'Be sure to come back tomorrow. You'll get your reward.'

'If I come back tomorrow it'll be only to see you, my lovely, I'll never forget your name . . . Ilona!'

She smiled and waited.

But John suddenly felt tongue-tied. He couldn't think of anything to say.

'I'll be back tomorrow,' he murmured and departed quickly.

On the way home he kept on invoking the image of the fairy queen in the white starched apron and murmured words of endearment. He was composing a love letter every word of which dazzled and sang, wooed and burned. He felt that he had never composed such a letter in his life – even though he was quite an expert.

By the time he got home, the letter was all finished, he only had to put it down on paper. He posted it next morning to Ilona Kincses. Then he waited. This time he was certain of success.

Yesterday he had only shown himself an honest finder – but this letter was going to prove his wit, his poetical mind, his love.

The reply came quickly – by return post. Orphan John tore open the envelope with trembling fingers and shivered as he read the rounded, childish script.

'My dear sir,
    Though your words have touched me to the core and

I wish I could answer them as you desire, a power greater than myself prevents me from giving you a favourable reply. The ways of love are mysterious indeed and I had already pledged my heart when fate made our paths converge. Accept the expressions of my most sincere regret and the hope that you won't deny your friendship in the future though . . . '

He stopped reading. The lines began to dance in front of his eyes. The words were so familiar! He reached into his pocket, took out 'HOW TO WRITE LOVE LETTERS' and thumbed through the pages until he came to the appendix. There he found Ilona's letter word for word, under the heading: 'Reply of refusal to a love letter by an over-familiar suitor.' His hopes and his pride collapsed in the same moment.

Do you agree, then, that there is poetic injustice in our world?

Boomerang

For twenty-five years, my friend Topliquet said, my wife has had the same hobby and preoccupation: to present paragons, to conjure up ideals, to set models for me to follow. Eight years ago Villaret managed to find a rent-controlled apartment in a garden suburb and became a solid basis of reference in our modest and rather crowded home during the regular, intimate but unfriendly dialogues we conduct. Villaret has acquired a sobriquet – he has become *How-Did-He-Do-It* Villaret or *How-Did-He* for short.

It is now five years since I have become alienated from my dear, old friend Achille Aumale – ever since he rose to be chairman of his firm, Mortmain and Mute, the fast-growing undertakers. He, too, had acquired an additional *epitheton ornans* (as the Greeks called it), the euphonius *Look-How-Far-He-Got*, sometimes shortened to *Look-How-Far*. I could also mention the *But-Of-Course*. The Sugarols, a couple who have just bought their second (or was it the third?) yacht. Then there is my wife's niece Penny or, to quote her full and well-deserved name, *She-Can-Afford-It (Why-Can't-We?)* referring to her family globe-trotting. The postcards which Penny sends us with, to my mind, reckless spendthrift abandon, are projected every evening by my wife upon my pillow – she has bought a rather expensive piece of apparatus for this purpose – before I can put down my weary head to rest.

After all this, I am sure you will understand how happy I was to meet an old school-chum a few weeks ago. It was at least twenty-five years since I saw François Galbert. We had a brief chat – but it was sufficient for me to take his arm and guide him round the square, straight up the stairs and into our apartment.

'This is François Galbert,' I presented him to my wife. 'We were together at school – I always considered him my model . . . Tell me,' I turned to François, 'how long is it since you first promised your wife to take her to India?'

'Eighteen years,' said Galbert gently. 'But something always cropped up . . .'

'And your wife understands?' I asked, raising my eyebrows significantly.

'Of course,' said Galbert affectionately, and smiled at my wife. 'What else could she do?' he added.

'Well, naturally,' said I and didn't even look at my wife. 'Where do you live now, François?'

'Don't you remember?' Galbert sounded surprised. 'At Ménilmontant.'

'Still in that awful, dark tenement, overlooking the gasworks?' I exclaimed in pretended surprise.

My friend was playing with the fringed tablecloth, pulling and twisting the fringes around his fingers.

'I must say,' he admitted, 'I've seen far better places. Plenty of them.'

'You see!' I told my wife and pointed at Galbert much as she used to point at Aumale or Villaret. 'You see! But of course, Galbert doesn't mind still living in the same old place. And your work?' I turned again to our guest.

'At Moody, Moody, Snide & Waste . . .'

'Really? but didn't you take that job as soon as you left school? By now, I am sure, you must be one of the senior partners.'

'Not exactly,' said François with a laugh as if I had told some brilliant joke. 'There are a few people ahead of me. But I can't complain. During the last five years they raised my salary twice – each time by two-and-a-half per cent.'

'Why don't you two have a nice long talk,' I said now. 'I'll make some tea.'

While the water boiled, I managed to extract from the hall closet our graduation daguerretype. I drew a red halo around Galbert's head and served it together with the tea and cake. Then I hung it on a nail in the living room.

'So I can see you all the time!' I told Galbert. 'A true

paragon!' I added and shook with silent laughter at my dear wife's expense. 'Tell me,' it occurred to me to ask, 'did you get your wife a new crinoline outfit yet?'

Galbert just shook his head, deeply ashamed.

'You must come again!' I shouted. 'And again and again! The more often the better! I insist. You'll find Helen always at home. Helen has always refused to take in work. Tell me, does your wife take in work? Can she afford to sit at home all day doing nothing like my Helen? Can Mrs François Galbert afford it?'

'That she can't,' said Galbert and gave my wife a long, sorrowful look.

Two weeks later Helen left me. It was only then that I found out: Galbert had called half-a-dozen times, for a 'friendly talk' with my wife – and she fell in love with him, madly, passionately. She took only a small suitcase and I was told by her solicitor that she did not want any of our communal property. All she carried away with her was our graduation daguerretype with Galbert and the halo around his head.

The School of Happiness

1

Valentine sat on a bench, hanging his head. Pigeons paraded in the dust; the young, sickly trees of the small square stood up straight in the evening dusk like the proud poor. The pink summer sky had faded above the grey church steeple. The square was nicknamed Place of Idle Hands.

Along the streets leading into the square people were busily bent on their private and bread-winning concerns. Valentine felt pensive. He lit a Russian cigarette – he was surprised that he still had some left – and went on brooding. He had almost decided to go to the zoo and talk to the Giant Sloth when someone stopped in front of him and asked, softly like a good fairy:

'Are you unhappy, sir?'

Valentine looked up. A young, well-dressed girl with a serious face stood in front of him. In his present mood he almost said something rude but changed his mind at the very last moment.

'Yes, I'm unhappy,' he replied indifferently.

'I'm sure you haven't graduated from the school of happiness,' said the young lady politely.

'What on earth . . . ' snorted Valentine.

'Happiness must be naturally studied and learned,' the girl declared 'Please, enroll at the school.'

Valentine inhaled deeply.

'I have no money for school-fees,' he explained curtly.

'It doesn't matter, sir,' said the girl. 'If you prove to be a good student, you will get a free scholarship . . . '

'Now, really,' Valentine protested, 'what sort of nonsense is this?'

'Excuse me,' the girl replied, 'you have no cause for complaint. I didn't ask you for anything – I merely made an offer.'

'All right, all right,' Valentine squeezed up his eyes, 'but I don't understand what the offer is about. After all, you don't accept a gift without knowing what it is – it can be dangerous or malignant . . .'

She kept silent, looking at him expectantly as if waiting for an explanation.

'Suppose you hand me an anarchist's bomb,' Valentine continued. 'I hold it for a few seconds and then I'm blown to smithereens . . .'

The girl smiled.

'Don't be so suspicious,' she admonished him. 'Why should I want to harm you? Come on, I'll take you to our lady principal.'

Valentine got to his feet slowly; he had lost his liking for argument and took the line of least resistance; he just followed the girl, silent, his hands in his pockets.

2

Valentine had never seen such a bare, dreary place as the room into which he was ushered. The walls, the ceiling, the stone floor were all of the same dazzling white colour; there wasn't a single break in this aggressive whiteness where the eye could rest. About ten people, all looking incredibly depressed, sat on white backless chairs. It was like a funeral congregation – except that they were being lectured by an ugly, wrinkled hunchback woman whose very voice was a shrill abomination.

She was sitting on a somewhat taller chair, held a book in her lap and cast now her strange, beady eyes upon the newcomers – Valentine and the girl.

'Welcome,' she piped and offered Valentine her hand. Valentine bowed and, overcoming his growing horror, touched the monkey paw of the lady principal.

'This gentleman was sitting in the Place of Idle Hands,' the young girl said – and disappeared.

'Sit down, please,' the old woman pointed to an empty stool.

Valentine obeyed.

'If you don't mind, I'll finish the lecture first – then we can talk,' said the old crone with a frightful smile and Valentine ducked. He would have given a lot for a way to escape. He had come to the place without any enthusiasm, hadn't expected anything favourable or pleasant – but what he found surpassed his worst fears. This must be complete lunacy. The miserable creatures on the backless chairs stared imploringly at the old woman. Was she a witch? Valentine had never seen such an unhappy crowd in his life – and this was called the School of Happiness! He gave the old woman an uneasy look. What was she lecturing about? For a moment he thought that perhaps she would speak of fabulously true and beautiful things; that all these sad faces would brighten, maybe there would be laughter and peace! He could hardly wait for her to start.

She did begin in a few seconds – and her words were even more awful than the place, her looks or the whole atmosphere.

Five minutes later Valentine was sitting with his face in his hands, sobbing like the others. The old woman spoke of the most terrible things, the most painful, tormenting elements of life – and she presented them in the darkest, most dramatic and amazingly vivid terms. Valentine covered his ears – but in vain. The voice continued inexorably. At last he couldn't stand it any longer, he jumped to his feet and started to shout while his whole body was racked by sobs and the tears were running down his face.

The old woman got up and tiptoed to him hurriedly.

'Forgive me,' she said politely. 'This is our second term class – the curriculum is too difficult for you. I'm the one to blame, I shouldn't have let you listen to my lecture . . . .'

She rang a bell and a nurse entered who ushered Valentine from the classroom. He was on the verge of collapse; he had never felt himself so unhappy in all his life. He was taken to a small room, made to sit down and given a glass of water to drink.

3

Next day he was once again sitting in the Place of Idle Hands. Once again he had a few cigarettes in his pocket and once again he had a different view of life.

The fat pigeons promenaded at his feet, nodding busily.

But suddenly someone stopped in front of him. The same girl who had taken him the day before to the School of Happiness.

'Leave me alone,' Valentine said angrily. I hope you don't want me to go back to that place?'

'Oh, but I do,' the young woman replied with insolent tranquillity.

Valentine could only stammer. After all the horrors he had experienced . . . how dare she . . . this was the limit . . .

'Yet it seems to me that you're already somewhat happier,' the girl said in a friendly tone. 'The School of Happiness has already helped you. A few more lessons and you'll become a happy man, sir. I'm quite sure of that.'

Valentine stared at her. 'Let me tell you, young lady, that I wouldn't go back to that ghastly place for all the money in the world. Yet I need money badly,' he added pensively.

The girl nodded. 'As you please. I can't force you.' She hesitated for a moment, then opened her handbag and gave Valentine a card. 'But if you ever decided you needed the School of Happiness, here's our address.'

Valentine pocketed the card unwillingly. He would have liked to tear it up – but didn't. The girl left – she practically melted away – and the card became dog-eared and yellowed in Valentine's pocket together with other bits of paper he was too lazy to throw away.

4

But one day there wasn't a single cigarette in his pockets. Once again he was sitting in the Place of Idle Hands but summer had gone a long time before. Valentine searched his pockets, hoping to find a crushed cigarette or maybe a coin or two he could use for buying some. He found bits of paper

– and among them the card with the address of the School of Happiness.

He stared at it for a long time and, inexplicably, felt an irresistible urge to go there. Where else could he go? He was apparently fated to study the subject, to finish a course...

The headmistress, the miniature monster, received him with a smile and enrolled him on the spot. Valentine became the most diligent student of the school. After a few months and almost incredible suffering, he received a diploma which declared that he was now qualified to face anything and anybody. He was thoroughly educated in the miseries of life and able to overcome them. According to the diploma he was a happy man; he had received such training in happiness that he spoke its language just as well as his own mother tongue; no one could spoil his happiness or rob him of it.

He faced the headmistress with shining eyes and when she offered him her hand, he kissed the tiny monkey paw.

'My dear boy,' said the fragile little horror, 'I'm very glad that I succeeded in making you happy...'

Valentine squared his shoulders and thought that now there was nothing in life he couldn't achieve. There was no obstacle that could stop him; no demand too heavy, no task too arduous. But before he left here was one question he wanted to ask.

'Madam,' he posed his final question, 'would you tell me what made you establish the School of Happiness?'

'Nothing simpler,' the headmistress said. 'It wasn't my original idea. It was a mere accident that led to the foundation of the school. Look at me. I'm a cripple. But that's not all. My father was a criminal, my mother a beggar woman. I hadn't a single good quality, a single asset in life. Nobody understood why God had put me into the world – the most miserable, most loathsome creature that ever lived.'

A single tear of happiness began to glide down her withered cheek.

'Until one day I discovered my mission in life. I told myself: I *must* be happy – and if I achieve happiness, this proves that everybody *can* be happy provided they acquire the necessary knowledge. If I, the most evil and despicable human being reach happiness, this means that happiness does not depend on anything. The bad and the painful things in life also serve happiness if you learn how to handle them. So one must only learn how to deal with suffering and ugliness, hate and outrage. This is the purpose of the School of Happiness.'

NEL BESTSELLERS

Crime

W002 773	THE LIGHT OF DAY	Eric Ambler	25p
W002 786	ABILITY TO KILL	Eric Ambler	25p
W002 799	THE MURDER LEAGUE	Robert L. Fish	30p
W002 876	MURDER MUST ADVERTISE	Dorothy L. Sayers	35p
W002 849	STRONG POISON	Dorothy L. Sayers	30p
W002 848	CLOUDS OF WITNESS	Dorothy L. Sayers	35p
W002 845	THE DOCUMENTS IN THE CASE	Dorothy L. Sayers	30p
W002 877	WHOSE BODY	Dorothy L. Sayers	30p
W002 749	THE NINE TAILORS	Dorothy L. Sayers	30p
W002 871	THE UNPLEASANTNESS AT THE BELLONA CLUB	Dorothy L. Sayers	30p
W002 750	FIVE RED HERRINGS	Dorothy L. Sayers	30p
W002 826	UNNATURAL DEATH	Dorothy L. Sayers	30p
W003 011	GAUDY NIGHT	Dorothy L. Sayers	40p
W002 870	BLOODY MAMA	Robert Thom	25p

Fiction

W002 755	PAID SERVANT	E. R. Braithwaite	30p
T005 801	RIFIFI IN NEW YORK	Auguste le Breton	30p
W002 833	THE CRAZY LADIES	Joyce Elbert	40p
W002 743	HARRISON HIGH	John Farris	40p
W002 861	THE GIRL FROM HARRISON HIGH	John Farris	40p
T007 030	A TIME OF PREDATORS	Joe Gores	30p
W002 424	CHILDREN OF KAYWANA	Edgar Mittelholzer	37½p
W002 425	KAYWANA STOCK	Edgar Mittelholzer	37½p
W002 426	KAYWANA BLOOD	Edgar Mittelholzer	37½p
T009 084	SIR, YOU BASTARD	G. F. Newman	30p
W002 881	THE FORTUNATE PILGRIM	Mario Puzo	35p
W002 752	THE HARRAD EXPERIMENT	Robert H. Rimmer	30p
W002 920	PROPOSITION 31	Robert H. Rimmer	30p
W002 427	THE ZOLOTOV AFFAIR	Robert H. Rimmer	25p
W002 704	THE REBELLION OF YALE MARRATT	Robert H. Rimmer	30p
W002 896	THE CARPETBAGGERS	Harold Robbins	75p
W002 918	THE ADVENTURERS	Harold Robbins	75p
W002 941	A STONE FOR DANNY FISHER	Harold Robbins	50p
W002 654	NEVER LOVE A STRANGER	Harold Robbins	60p
W002 653	THE DREAM MERCHANTS	Harold Robbins	60p
W002 917	WHERE LOVE HAS GONE	Harold Robbins	60p
W002 155	NEVER LEAVE ME	Harold Robbins	25p
T006 743	THE INHERITORS	Harold Robbins	60p
T009 467	STILETTO	Harold Robbins	30p
W002 761	THE SEVEN MINUTES	Irving Wallace	75p
W002 580	THE BEAUTIFUL COUPLE	William Woolfolk	37½p
W002 312	BRIDE OF LIBERTY	Frank Yerby	25p
W002 479	AN ODOUR OF SANCTITY	Frank Yerby	50p
W002 916	BENTON'S ROW	Frank Yerby	40p
W002 822	GILLIAN	Frank Yerby	40p
W002 895	CAPTAIN REBEL	Frank Yerby	30p
W003 010	THE VIXENS	Frank Yerby	40p
W003 007	A WOMAN CALLED FANCY	Frank Yerby	30p

Science Fiction

T009 696	GLORY ROAD	Robert Heinlein	40p
W002 844	STRANGER IN A STRANGE LAND	Robert Heinlein	60p
W002 386	PODKAYNE OF MARS	Robert Heinlein	30p
W002 449	THE MOON IS A HARSH MISTRESS	Robert Heinlein	40p
W002 630	THE MAN WHO SOLD THE MOON	Robert Heinlein	30p
W002 754	DUNE	Frank Herbert	60p
W002 911	SANTAROGA BARRIER	Frank Herbert	30p
W002 641	NIGHT WALK	Bob Shaw	25p
W002 716	SHADOW OF HEAVEN	Bob Shaw	25p

War

W002 686	DEATH OF A REGIMENT	John Foley	30p
W002 484	THE FLEET THAT HAD TO DIE	Richard Hough	25p
W002 805	HUNTING OF FORCE Z	Richard Hough	30p
W002 494	P.Q. 17—CONVOY TO HELL	Lund Ludlam	25p
W002 423	STROKE FROM THE SKY—THE BATTLE OF BRITAIN STORY	Alexandra McKee	30p
W002 471	THE STEEL COCOON	Bentz Plagemann	25p
W002 831	NIGHT	Francis Pollini	40p

Western

Walt Slade—Bestsellers

W002 634	THE SKY RIDERS	Bradford Scott	20p
W002 648	OUTLAW ROUNDUP	Bradford Scott	20p
W002 649	RED ROAD OF VENGEANCE	Bradford Scott	20p
W002 669	BOOM TOWN	Bradford Scott	20p
W002 687	THE RIVER RAIDERS	Bradford Scott	20p

General

W002 420	THE SECOND SEX	Simone De Beauvoir	42½p
W002 234	SEX MANNERS FOR MEN	Robert Chartham	25p
W002 531	SEX MANNERS FOR ADVANCED LOVERS	Robert Chartham	25p
W002 766	SEX MANNERS FOR THE YOUNG GENERATION	Robert Chartham	25p
W002 835	SEX AND THE OVER FORTIES	Robert Chartham	30p
T007 006	THE CHARTHAM LETTERS	Robert Chartham	30p
P002 367	AN ABZ OF LOVE	Inge and Sten Hegeler	60p
W002 369	A HAPPIER SEX LIFE (Illustrated)	Dr. Sha Kokken	60p
W002 136	WOMEN	John Philip Lundin	25p
W002 333	MISTRESSES	John Philip Lundin	25p
T007 022	THE NEW FEMALE SEXUALITY	Manfred F. De Martino	50p
W002 859	SMOKEWATCHERS HOW TO QUIT BOOK	Smokewatchers Group	25p
W002 584	SEX MANNERS FOR SINGLE GIRLS	Dr. G. Valensin	25p
W002 592	THE FRENCH ART OF SEX MANNERS	Dr. G. Valensin	25p

Mad

S003 702	A MAD LOOK AT OLD MOVIES	25p
S003 523	BOILING MAD	25p
S003 496	THE MAD ADVENTURES OF CAPTAIN KLUTZ	25p
S003 719	THE QUESTIONABLE MAD	25p
S003 714	FLIGHTING MAD	25p
S003 613	HOWLING MAD	25p
S003 477	INDIGESTIBLE MAD	25p
S004 163	THE MAD BOOK OF MAGIC	25p
S004 304	MAD ABOUT MAD	25p

- - - - - - - - - - - - - - - -

NEL P.O. BOX 11 FALMOUTH CORNWALL

Please send cheque or postal order. Allow 5p per book to cover postage and packing (Overseas 6p per book).

Name ....

Address ....

....

Title ....
(JULY)